Corporate Mandated Holiday Romance

Nellie Wilson

To Elle & Yaffa – for answering all of my questions for almost two decades.
Put a bird on it.

Copyright © 2023 by Nellie Wilson

Cover Art by Kelsey Bowman at Let's Get Lit Studio

All rights reserved.

No portion of this book may be reproduced in any form without written permission from the publisher or author, except as permitted by U.S. copyright law.

Contents

Author's Note	VII
1. Chapter 1	1
2. Chapter 2	6
3. Chapter 3	11
4. Chapter 4	16
5. Chapter 5	23
6. Chapter 6	31
7. Chapter 7	40
8. Chapter 8	47
9. Chapter 9	55
10. Chapter 10	65
11. Chapter 11	72
12. Chapter 12	82
13. Chapter 13	90
14. Chapter 14	96

15.	Chapter 15	107
16.	Chapter 16	117
17.	Chapter 17	125
18.	Chapter 18	131
19.	Chapter 19	138
20.	Chapter 20	144
21.	Chapter 21	153
22.	Chapter 22	163
23.	Chapter 23	169
24.	Chapter 24	172
25.	Chapter 25	183
26.	Chapter 26	186
27.	Chapter 27	193
28.	Chapter 28	195
29.	Chapter 29	204
30.	Epilogue	207
	Acknowledgements	210
	About Nellie	212
	Also By Nellie Wilson	213

Author's Note

Thank you for picking up this copy of *Corporate Mandated Holiday Romance*. This book was born out of wonderful conversations with friends of mine, my extreme dislike of the fact billionaires exist, and my desire to write a Christmas book with a Nellie Wilson twist. The billionaire is *not* the love interest; a nerdy journalist named Max is. There are a few content warnings I'd like you to be aware of: consumption of alcohol and a lecherous boss.

Max is Jewish; I am not. This is the primary reason this book is in first person POV, as I don't feel like it is my place to write as a Jewish character. However, from the early days of drafting, I have benefitted from the advice and critique of Jewish sensitivity consultants, many of whom I've been lucky to call my friends for years. Any mistakes, however, are my own.

Please continue to stand up for justice in your own communities. I wrote this book as a reminder of the power of one person speaking up when they notice something wrong.

Much love,

Nellie

Chapter 1

"Wakey, wakey, eggs and bakey!" My roommate, Gemma, barges into my room at the ungodly hour of six a.m., waving a piece of crispy bacon in front of her. Jokes on her, though. I've been up since around three thirty, the time on my phone taunting me every time I looked at it hoping that I could rewind time and fall asleep. Or, alternatively, speed it up and time jump to when I needed to wake up.

"Ugnh," I reply elegantly, rolling over and smashing my face in my pillows. Gemma comes closer, dangling the bacon about three inches in front of my nose.

"You love bacon, Brooklyn," she says. I open my mouth, hoping to snag a bite, but she pulls it away from me at the last minute. "Get your ass out of bed, and you'll get some."

I mumble some other noises and make sure to tuck in some swear words to let Gemma know how I really feel about her bacon feint, then look over toward my tiny closet, where my first-day-of-work outfit has been laid out for the past week. Because today is the day. The day where I finally get a chance to live my silly little-girl dream.

You know how every little kid has dreams, right? Ridiculous careers like dolphin trainer or president or tomb raider (hey, Lara Croft was an icon). Ever since I was a little girl, I wanted to save the rainforest and the whales and figure out a way to sew up the hole in the ozone layer. I carried around brightly colored notebooks covered in neon tigers and leopards, thinking about the ways that my own impacts affected these landscapes thousands of miles away. I bothered my mom and stepdad about the way they left the sink running while they brushed their teeth. I hounded my sister in high school when she wouldn't buy a reusable water bottle, claiming that the Evian bottles looked iconic. Hell, I even cried when I realized that where I grew up—the San Fernando Valley of Los Angeles—should have been a desert and the entire growth of Los Angeles was predicated on stolen water from farmers hundreds of miles to the north. I dreamed of being a member of the Planeteers and saving the planet.

Today I get to live that dream.

Well, in a way. Like the dreams of the vast majority of my generation, those of us who came of age during the post-9/11 era and went to college during the first of what would be multiple recessions during our lives, mine were popped by the reality of student loans and practicality. Instead of becoming an environmental scientist, I went into marketing after receiving a boring, beige degree in business. I've spent more than a decade caring about SEO and branding, thinking about the ways that various companies can target ads toward people who need to be excited by a new kind of dish soap.

However, a few months ago, I received a message via my LinkedIn (a website that I, unfortunately, have to care about) regarding a job opening at a company that was everything I admired. Not only did they work in sustainable waste disposal, but they were run by the man that I've idealized since college. A professor had shown us a TED

Talk by Aron Callahan, a young CEO who was changing the game. He had openly talked about the need to diversify the environmental consulting field and discussed ways to make the work environment as close to zero waste as possible. I fell in love that very day and followed his career and the rise of ConservTech through all the Forbes and *Times* features. I memorized nearly every op-ed he published in the last decade, thinking about the ways I could be the most environmentally responsible employee. He donated his yearly salary to Planned Parenthood one year and spoke out about how his company would pay for gender affirming care for any staff member. He was constantly speaking to business conventions and summits of world leaders about the ways in which corporations could partner with governments to help meet climate goals.

It didn't hurt that he was absolutely gorgeous.

I wonder if I'll ever catch a glimpse of him in the office.

Buttoning up my blouse, I take a look at myself in the mirror. Wide-legged pants, a breezy blouse with a cardigan for the Los Angeles fall (or, more likely, an office that I imagine doesn't' spend much money on heat). I add just enough makeup—all organic—to make it look like I've slept and I know what I'm doing and a bit of highlighter on my cheeks. I've got wavy brown hair that I decide to pull up into a twist, leaving two strands framing my face in a more mature version of the way I wore it every day in middle school. I opt for heels, needing every bit of confidence to bump my five-foot-three height to something near average.

Gemma wolf whistles from where she's stationed at the stove as I head into the kitchen. I give a spin and flick my foot into the air, and she laughs and rewards me with a piece of bacon.

"Ready for day one?" she asks, flipping an omelet with the ease that comes from her stint in culinary school. Gemma is decidedly undecided in how she approaches her life. In the past five years since we moved in together, she's worked as a chef, a bar manager, an organizer for in-home Botox parties, and a coordinator for red-carpet events in Santa Monica. Currently, she's going back to school for a degree in fashion merchandising while bartending. I adore her chaos.

"As ready as I can be," I reply, pouring myself a cup of coffee. "Hopefully all of my years of boring-ass office jobs will finally pay off." The only arguments Gemma and I have ever had, other than the occasional dust-up over who's going to take the recycling down the hall to the trash room, were about her insistence that I've been selling myself short by taking boring office job after boring office job. But I'm not Gemma. Gemma, who has never once thought about the sunk cost fallacy or student loans by virtue of a wealthy grandmother who left her a trust fund and artist parents who allowed her to move out when she was sixteen to "find herself." A bit different from me: Brooklyn Peters, one of two children who grew up in a boring-ass subdivision and whose biggest adventure was one semester studying abroad in Italy in college. Brooklyn Peters, who dreamed of swimming with whale sharks or working with Steve Irwin and, instead, gets excited when an office has a new flavor of sparkling water.

Brooklyn Peters, newest employee of ConservTech.

"Should I drive or take the Metro today?" I ask Gemma as she scoops the omelet and more bacon onto my plate.

"Where's the office?"

"Century City."

"How's traffic?"

I take a peek at my phone. "It's not bad. I checked last night. It only takes, like, fifteen minutes to get there." Fifteen minutes to get anywhere in Los Angeles is a damn miracle.

"I'm proud of you, baby," Gemma says, handing me a paper lunch sack.

"Thanks, mom," I joke.

Gemma's face grows serious. "No, I know what this means to you. I know that I'm always on your case, but apparently, I'm eating my hat right now. This company matters, yeah?"

"Yeah," I reply. I love arguing about the design of advertisements and the polishing of final reports, but knowing that it will mean something more than just shareholders' bottom line? My blood is buzzing.

"Drive safe!" Gemma says as I grab my keys.

"It's fifteen minutes, grandma," I respond, rolling my eyes. "I've been driving around this city since I was sixteen, I'll be fine."

Chapter 2

I should know better than to trust that the trickster gods that manage LA traffic would be on my side. I didn't even have to get on a major highway, but I still spent most of my drive watching my speedometer range from five to ten miles an hour. I double checked the address of the new office building, but the parking lot was closed, so I spent another ten minutes looping the block, looking for a spot, which I had to parallel park into, so there's no way that I don't have pit stains on my blouse. Walking there is the next issue. I put new shoes on without breaking them in because "who even walks in Los Angeles?" Now I'm dealing with two blisters on my left foot. By the time I get to the six-story glass building, I'm sweating, my hair is a mess, and I'm sure my mascara has run and my eyeliner is gone. I expect a moment of peace and clarity when I see the building that matches the address on my phone, but I just feel sticky and late. Taking another glimpse at the sparse email the company sent, I confirm I'm right. I've got an address, a username, and a temporary password, but I assume that the company has a good onboarding program. Hopefully with snacks.

CORPORATE MANDATED HOLIDAY ROMANCE

Century City is an interesting choice for a company that prides itself on promoting adaptive reuse of old buildings. Everything around me feels both new and old, like I can imagine people smoking at their desks, but it would also smell like fresh drywall. I walk into the lobby, head held high, regardless of how cold and miserable my coffee is.

"Hi," I say brightly to the security guard. "I'm here for ConservTech? I'm a new employee?" I mentally curse myself for my stupid upspeak—the faint trace of the Valley accent that I can't seem to shake no matter how hard I try.

"Fifth floor," he responds, barely looking up from the replay of last night's Dodgers game on his phone next to the security camera.

"Thanks?" I hoist my bag higher on my shoulder and realize that I've probably got a sweat stain from the handle on my blouse. Shit.

"Good luck," he snorts. I can't tell whether he's talking to the Dodgers or to me. As I usually do, I choose to assume that he's talking to the game or that he's had a bad day. Maybe he got decaf coffee by accident this morning.

I walk over to the elevator and hit the up arrow, then step through the gold doors. After pressing the button printed with the number 5, I dig into my bag and pull my cardigan on, because the lobby is *freezing*. And I wait.

And wait.

And wait.

And finally notice that there's a place to swipe a keycard or a badge to access the higher floors.

I do not have said keycard or badge.

I don't like looking stupid, so I can't go back into the lobby and interrupt that guy watching baseball. Plus, he seemed grumpy.

I decide just to wait. I'm not technically due at the office for another fifteen minutes, and I'm sure someone is going to come into the elevator soon. Some lovely, kind secretary. One who wears pearl earrings and a matching brooch. Her name is Helen. Or Mary. Maybe she has a little bit of a southern accent. Calls you "darling," but it doesn't seem offensive. She bakes cookies for the office and makes everyone look at photos of her grandchildren.

I feel comforted already. The doors open, and I'm ready to be welcomed by Francine.

The outline of the person in front of me is most definitely *not* Helen-Mary-Francine.

He is tall. And broad shouldered. And in a suit that looks like every stitch was perfectly calculated for his body. Which, looking at the type of shoes on his feet, it probably was. I look up to make confident eye contact, and I'm stunned.

And look, with the exception of the six months in Florence where I did my best to replace my blood with red wine, I've lived in Los Angeles my entire life. People here are gorgeous, mostly because everyone you see in this image-obsessed town was the prettiest person from their small town before they moved here to make it. Beautiful people in Los Angeles are a bit like the drone of traffic—you don't notice it after a few days, and it becomes white noise in the background.

But this man? *Whoa*. He's got a jaw line that would make a Kennedy blush, a five-o'clock shadow that's perfectly trimmed, and a straight nose that tells me he can afford to have it fixed. His hair is dark and curled at the ends with just a hint of gel, which complements steely gray eyes that have annoyingly long lashes. He gives off the vibe of having gone to a boarding school and then to an Ivy—the type of privilege that doesn't open doors so much as blast them down.

He pushes his sunglasses into his hair and stares at me.

"Good morning?" I squeak.

"Do you not know how to work an elevator?" he asks with a dismissive air. For some stupid reason, I immediately and automatically crave his approval.

"I, uh, don't have a keycard yet," I gesture vaguely at the elevator buttons. "It's my first day in the building."

"And your company didn't see fit to have you ready to hit the ground running?" He pulls out his own card and waves it in front of the reader, followed by a dismissive sniff.

"Sadly not," I say, reaching across his arm to tap the button for floor five. "Or maybe they did, but I was too excited this morning and misread my email?" Benefit of the doubt, always. "I'm really excited to work here." I cringe internally, knowing that there are probably two dozen companies that rent space in this building. I clamp my mouth shut so I don't say anything else stupid as the elevator doors close and we're moved swiftly to the top. I can feel him looking at me, and I look down at my J. Crew outfit paired with my Target shoes. I hope I look enough like a professional. After getting the job, I went on a small shopping spree at the Santa Monica mall Working remotely for five years meant that I had defaulted to leggings, tank tops, and hoodies as my work outfits. The hiring manager here was insistent that the company was like a family, and families worked together. Plus "Mr. Callahan" believed in the importance of face-to-face interaction for all departments. I would have taken the job even if I had to drive to Orange County every single day.

Actually, come to think of it, this *man* looks an awful lot like Aron. He hasn't done many public interviews in a few years, so my mental picture is based mostly on one specific TED Talk I've watched so many times I can quote it word for word. He's got the same jaw and similar hair, but most white men in Los Angeles who look vaguely corporatey. Plus, this man has none of the warmth that Aron—Mr. Callahan now,

I guess, as he is my boss—exudes in his interviews. It's hard to imagine how the iceman standing next to me who's tapping angrily away on his phone while flashing a Rolex the size of my fist could donate his entire salary to fund reproductive health care.

The elevator gives a soft chime that signals that I'm on my floor. I move to get off, and I have the horrifying realization that I never asked him what floor he needed. I ignored elevator etiquette 101. However, he sweeps past me in a moment of coincidence.

Manners crisis averted, I give a weird wave and say thank you, wishing him a good day.

I end up following him off the elevator and into the hallway as he makes a turn to the right. At least I remembered that direction from my initial email.

I follow him until he stops in front of double glass doors with *ConservTech* on them. Shit, I'll have to run into this man around the office, and he'll forever know me as Idiot Elevator Girl. I make the quick decision to hang back for a few moments, to look at my phone or fix my shoe. I'm close enough, however, to hear the secretary greet him.

"Good morning, Mr. Callahan." Her voice sounds a bit hesitant, as if she wasn't expecting him.

No.

Shit.

It can't be, right? I wait a breath, then two, and decide to make my entrance, hoping he's gone and I've misheard her.

He's not. He's standing at the desk, under a high-quality portrait of himself adorned with a gold plaque that reads *Aron Callahan, Founder and CEO*.

I should probably just quit now.

Chapter 3

"This is the company that didn't ensure a new hire was properly equipped for her first day?" Aron, Mr. Callahan, my idol, says to me. His steel eyes bounce up and down my body, then slide over to the receptionist. "Brenda, why was this new employee—" he pauses and looks back at me, waiting for me to fill the silence.

"Brooklyn," I add. "Brooklyn Peters."

"Brenda, why was Brooklyn not prepared for her first day here?"

I give what I hope is a sympathetic smile to her while she furiously clacks away at her computer.

"Mr. Callahan, I sent her an email with all the instructions and she filled out all of the pre-hire paperwork and legal agreements—" she begins, but Aron smacks his hand on the desk to silence her. That's the first unattractive thing he's done, and it reminds me of the way that my mom's ex-boyfriend would snap at waitresses when he wanted a check quickly. Something hot and acidic simmers in my stomach.

"Unacceptable." His voice has dropped to a whisper, but I would rather he was yelling. "We are an employee-first company, Brenda." He fixes her with a steady glare. "Don't do it again."

"Yes, sir," she replies, then she goes back to clicking her mouse. I mouth an apology to her and whisper, "I didn't know." She gives me a half-hearted smile in return and shakes her head. *You know how men are*, she seems to say.

Don't I know it. My mom shuffled through the cream of the crop of the douchebags of Greater Los Angeles before meeting my stepdad and I've had too many first dates that go nowhere to count. I'm not writing off *all* men, of course, but my mom and I seem to have a special kind of homing beacon for assholes.

"Brooklyn." Aron—Mr. Callahan—says my name as a complete sentence. It sounds like a command.

"Yes?"

"What department are you in?"

"Marketing?"

"Are you sure about that?" he asks. I can't tell if he's joking or not, so I decide to assume he is.

"I'm sure that Brenda can get me all set up." She seems friendly.

"I doubt that after how today has gone so far," he replies. "I'll show you to your desk." Another sentence that isn't a request, and he begins walking with the assurance that Brenda and I won't challenge him. "I'd like to ensure the rest of your first day at my company goes better than your first five minutes." He looks over his shoulder at Brenda, and I begin to feel like I need to defend this woman. She remains nonplussed, her face falling into a half smile that tells me this might be a typical Tuesday for her.

"Mr. Callahan, really, it's fine. I'm sure you're busy—"

"Aron," he interjects.

"Mr. Callahan," I repeat, doubtful that the author of my favorite employment blog would write an advice column about starting day one by calling the CEO by his first name.

CORPORATE MANDATED HOLIDAY ROMANCE   13

"Aron," he repeats, a bit more intensely. I like it a little more than I should. "You met me in the elevator as someone in the building. You met me as Aron, not Mr. Callahan." He gives me a smirk that I think is meant to travel straight between my legs, but it hits my stomach instead, making me a bit queasy.

"Oh, all right. Well, Aron, thank you, but I'm sure you have a billion things on your plate."

"Nonsense." And he's already walking past the front desk and down the maze of cubicles. I follow, keeping my eyes firmly above his waist, though I do notice how his suit jacket pulls in a really delicious manner.

Focus, Brooklyn.

He turns a few corners, and I'm feeling like I should have channeled Hansel and Gretel and left a trail of gluten-free breadcrumbs for when it's time to leave, but finally, we reach a glass-walled office equipped with five large desks. Each one is outfitted with the fanciest new computer. I breathe a sigh of relief when I catch sight of the two people here. They look like *my* people. I recognize the blouse one is wearing from last summer's Target sales rack. I own the same one.

"Marketing." Both sets of eyes dart up at Aron's greeting. I take notice of the way that their expressions flare in surprise and then harden. Tiny shifts of body language, like they're preparing for a fight, but with a tinge of *here we go again*. I want to open a composition notebook right now, *Harriet the Spy* style, and begin piecing together the office politics puzzle. I'm nervous again, but I remind myself of the company's mission, of the way that the entire recruiting and hiring process emphasized the company's commitment to sustainability. It's worth all of it.

"Yes, Mr. Callahan? Do you have an issue with next quarter's portfolio design we sent out?" This from the person who is nearest to me.

They're stunning in an androgynous manner—hair buzzed close to the scalp and earrings that look like leaves hanging from their ears.

"No, that was acceptable. This is Brooklyn Peters. It's her first day. I hope that you'll show her the welcome that I expect from everyone here."

"Brooklyn, I'll be seeing you around. Expect a meeting invitation on your calendar." With that, he turns on his heel, and I'm left feeling like the new kid who moved to school in the middle of November.

"Hi." I give a half-hearted wave. "I'm Brooklyn. You may have heard it's my first day."

"I'm Vee," the person with the shaved head says. "This is Carlina." They point to their companion. "Welcome to the team. Sorry that you were greeted by the reincarnation of Grumpy Cat."

"Grumpy Cat was adorable," Carlina argues, walking back to her desk and taking a sip of an iced coffee. "There is nothing adorable about Aron Callahan."

"Don't sass me, Carlina," Vee says in a decent impersonation of Mr. Callahan. Carlina rolls her eyes.

"Your desk is over there, next to Vee," Carlina says, pointing to an empty desk with a computer and a folder of documents on it. "We try to keep most things paperless, but I printed out all of your login info for the first day."

"Also, one time we had someone screw up their login on the first day, and Callahan fired them," Vee adds.

"Don't listen to them." Carlina waves a hand. "We've had trouble keeping a consistent team, and we're both really excited that you're here."

"A lot of work?" I ask, hopeful. I like being busy.

"Something like that," Vee says. "Or more like nothing we do is ever good enough, and eventually people get sick of being treated like shit."

"I mean, it's pretty neat that the CEO himself works in the same office, right?" I'm grasping at straws.

"Yeah, so he can keep his nose in everybody's business and remind us all that we could be fired at any time," Carlina replies, shifting her glasses to the top of her head.

"Carlina is a grump. It's part of her appeal. You'll get used to it, just like everything else here," Vee says with a friendly grin. "Welcome to the team."

I've never had a welcome quite like this.

Chapter 4

After shuffling my painfully blistered feet back to my car to find, of course, a parking ticket, I make it home in a relatively normal amount of time. I'm looking forward to plopping my ass on the couch and figuring out what reality show that focuses on the problems of the 1 percent I can rot my mind with. Vee and Carlina were lovely, and I have a good feeling about working with them. But Aron Callahan is decidedly not what I expected, and when I said goodbye to Brenda on the way out, she jumped and gave me a tentative wave, like she was afraid of messing up again. If I believed in trusting my intuition, I'd think something was wrong. But it could just be a bad day. Maybe Mr. Callahan was stuck in traffic, too. Maybe a client was rude to Brenda.

Anyway, I unlock the door to find Gemma talking to a stranger, and my shoulders slump. I've already met too many people today, and I'm not ready for another one of Gemma's new friends or new partners to be in my face.

That's the thing. Gemma is one of those people who hated being stuck in her house and started living twice as hard after COVID restrictions lifted. I *used* to be like that, used to go out with coworkers and swipe on men on apps, but when we all cocooned at home, I found that not many people reached out. Most of my friends were work friends, and when we went and stayed remote, we lost any excuse to keep hanging out. It was another reason I was looking forward to this new job.

"Hey, Brooklyn!" Gemma waves. And because she's Gemma, she knows me. "I ordered dinner!" She shifts to the side to reveal a plastic takeout container full of steaming noodles. Still not acknowledging the man in our kitchen, I grab a fork and shovel the pad Thai into my mouth.

"Is this a *whoo* pad Thai bite or an *oh fuck* pad Thai bite?" Gemma asks.

I swallow.

"Yeah," I respond.

"Sorry, Brooklyn. This is Max. He's my ex's brother and needed to pick up something that Lina left here," Gemma says, looking at him. I'm so exhausted that it takes until this moment to really look at him. He's tall and lanky and wearing a dark blue sweater and thin glasses.

"Hi," I say awkwardly.

"Hey," he responds.

"Sorry," I apologize. "First day at a new job. I'm exhausted."

"Congrats," he replies in a standard exchange. This is another reason I don't miss being out around people. Small talk is weird as hell. I expect to take my food and head to the other room, but he asks a question. "What do you do?"

"Oh, it's nothing. I work in marketing for an environmental company."

His eyes flash wide and then narrow slightly behind his glasses. "Which company?"

"ConservTech?" My voice goes up at the end, like I don't know where I work.

Max makes a disgruntled noise and purses his lips. "Oy vey," he says.

"Huh?"

"Just keep your eyes open and be careful. Don't find yourself alone in an office with the CEO," he says cryptically. *Who the fuck is this guy and how does he know anything?* I'm about to ask that question when Gemma comes back in holding a sweatshirt.

"Here," she says, passing it over. "I don't know why Lina needs it."

"Something about a theme party," Max says. "Thanks for keeping it."

"Well, it's a damn comfortable sweatshirt," Gemma replies. "You can leave now."

"Toodles," Max says. He gives her a wave and smiles at me, then he walks out the door. I'm not proud of the way my gaze follows his back and drops down to his slim waist.

"How did he find you?" Knowing Gemma, they go to the same astrologer or speakeasy.

"Lina and I still text. She moved to Colorado after we broke up, but we still send memes back and forth." Gemma grins at me. "It's a lesbian thing."

"I'd never talk to my ex-boyfriends," I comment half-heartedly.

"Eh, it's fine. How was day one?" Gemma grabs her own Thai food and a bottle of discount grocery story wine, and we head over to the couch.

"Not great," I hedge.

"Not great how?"

"Like, *my coworkers hate me and I think the CEO hit on me and also he's an asshole and I feel weird all the time* not good." I take a generous gulp of wine, knowing that even one full glass will be too much for me.

"I need more details." Gemma is practically salivating as I explain the entire day.

"Whoa, whoa, whoa. So Hot Elevator Guy is your idol?" she asks.

I nod to confirm.

"And he's a douche?"

I nod again.

"And you think he made a pass at you?"

I nod a third time.

"Well, that's certainly a conversation to have with HR during the rest of your onboarding."

"I can't bring this up!" I say, dropping my fork. "What if it's nothing? What if I misread the situation? I mean, there's a very real chance that he's just sitting there and hanging out, and I'm the weird one." I reach for the wine and take a gulp that hits funny, burning in my esophagus.

Gemma taps her chin, thinking. "You know who you could ask?"

"If you say to call your ex and have her read my tarot, the answer is no," I respond, fixing her with a hard glare.

"No." Gemma rolls her eyes. She taps a bit on her phone and gets a look on her face that terrifies me.

"This is the scheming face that you got when you suggested we try to sneak into that movie premiere."

"Yeah, but I also made out with a C-list actor who used to be on Disney Channel and did interviews about their purity ring when we were in high school, so that's a win," Gemma excitedly taps on her phone, and mine buzzes on the counter.

I roll my eyes. "What did you send me?"

"Max's contact info. The guy who was just here. I followed him on social media when I moved here and knew no one. He's one of those random people that always pops up on my feed, and he's a journalist. He specializes in corporate environmental reporting—I remember he did this article on the amount of cardboard used for next-day shipping instead of packaging items together—anyway, well. Here he is." A social media profile is on her screen.

She passes me her phone and gets up to get more wine while I scroll through. There are no photos, nothing that I would expect from the social media of anyone I know. Accounts out here are all about building a brand, something that everyone does, which means that my feed is a lot of photos of people's faces next to iconic Los Angeles places that none of us actually go to. But this page is just screenshots of news headlines.

CFO Found Supporting Logging Industry in Amazon

Local City Councilman's Campaign for Mayor Supported by Offshore Oil Lobby

Inside the Controversial World of Cross-State Agricultural Smuggling

I could keep scrolling, because there are dozens of stories, but my eye catches on one, a headline from before the pandemic.

Is Aron Callahan hiding for a reason?

I had chalked up Aron's avoiding of the press to a focus on his work. Something about how being named to *Time*'s 30 under 30 when he was twenty-five was a distraction from the real mission of ConservTech. But I've met him now. The man basically preens when anyone is near him, and I didn't miss the way his hand lingered on my shoulder or low back, the way that was too close when he explained the company's depth chart to me.

"Do you have his number?"

She takes her phone back and scrolls again, then my phone buzzes with a new message. "I never thought I'd see the day when I'd be setting you up with a guy."

I roll my eyes. "It's for work. And it's probably nothing. I think I spent too much time watching multi-part documentaries during lockdown." I mean, really. To hide in plain sight is just stupid. And Aron Callahan is not stupid. My brain can't square that circle. Because that would mean that I spent my twenties idealizing an idiot. I already did the whole *cover my walls with posters of football and baseball players* thing. This was supposed to represent me maturing.

I take another sip of wine, then put the mug down. I still have to work tomorrow, as much as everything about the first day unsettles me.

"I'm going to bed," I tell Gemma, scraping my pad Thai back into the takeout box and putting it in the fridge for lunch tomorrow. "Do you work tomorrow night?" She nods, tapping away on an app. "Okay, well, I'll make dinner and leave leftovers for you."

"Have fun texting Max," she calls as I walk into my bedroom. I change into a sweatshirt and shorts, brush my teeth, and take a vitamin I bought from a targeted ad. My usual routine before an average night's sleep and a typical day at work tomorrow. I'll *manifest it*, just like a training at my old job tried to tell me to do, or like the spin instructor at Soul Cycle screams to me as she sweats out cocaine and vodka.

It was just a weird first day. I was nervous, so I interpreted everything wrong. It was like the time I waited in line to meet my favorite boy band at the Galleria in Glendale. Five hours with my best friend Katie, each of us taking turns running to Auntie Anne's or Orange Julius to get snacks and refreshments while the other held the place in line. When I finally saw them, in all their frosted-tips and shiny-shirt glory, I held out the poster I bought at FYE and no words came out of my mouth. My brain went completely offline. Nothing. Too nervous to even say "I love your songs" or confess which one I thought was the cutest.

Yeah, I rationalize to myself. I was just nervous. That's why it was weird.

Chapter 5

I double-check traffic three times before I leave the house and make sure that the parking garage is open today. Day two has to be better than day one.

I'm frustrated to find out that the parking lot in my building is *not* free for employees. I'm struggling through the mental math and justice of how it can be eighty dollars a day to park here in the elevator from the below-ground parking garage when the elevator dings on the lobby floor. And, of course, Aron walks in, smelling like wealth and privilege and just a hint of sex.

I smell like Target brand shampoo and the leftover Thai food in the reusable Target bag I'm holding.

"Brooklyn Peters," Aron says, his voice low enough to register on the Richter scale. "Looking good today. And you figured out the elevator." He laughs, and his eyes shift down to my chest.

"Good morning, Mr. Callahan," I reply, shifting awkwardly.

"What did I tell you to call me?" He lifts an eyebrow.

"Good morning, Aron," I correct.

"Good girl," he replies. He smirks at me in the mirror of the elevator. While those words have definitely worked for me in...certain adult films I've watched before, I have to work to not pull a face. There's something that feels demeaning about it here, when I'm a professional. From my employer, no less. "What are you working on today?"

"I mean, it's day two! I'll see what Carlina and Vee could use help with."

"Who?"

"The other members of the marketing department." He was just there yesterday, talking to them...

"Right. Well." His eyes flicker to the bag I'm holding. "Could I take you to lunch today?"

I hold up my bag. "I've got leftovers." In my mind, this is an easy way to say no without, well, telling the head of my company no. It's money saving. Sustainable, even. Food waste is a major contributor to Los Angeles' gross trash output. I wrote a paper in college about how health and safety laws could be changed to encourage more reuse.

"Toss them," he responds. "Come have lunch at Café Gratitude with me. I'm sure it's better than whatever ethnic food is in that bag." He gives an over dramatic sniff.

"I'm good," I reply. "I really like Thai food."

"Suit yourself. I think you're missing a phenomenal opportunity to help your career. To get to know the...depths...of our practice here," he replies as the elevator opens on the fifth floor. "I'll see you around, Brooklyn." I nearly sprint off the elevator to the marketing department, which, thankfully, is on the other side of the floor from the CEO's office. Carlina and Vee are debating hard kombucha brands when I get in.

"What about you, Long Island?" Carlina asks.

"It's Brooklyn," I respond.

"She knows," Vee says in a stage whisper. "Just name your favorite hard kombucha."

"I'm not sure," I respond. "I'm not really much of a drinker?"

Carlina holds her hand to her chest, and Vee mimics a swoon that's worthy of a period drama's fainting couch. "A travesty! A young, beautiful woman such as yourself in Los Angeles without a favorite kombucha!"

"I'm from the Valley," I reply.

"That explains it," Vee deadpans.

"We're heading for a post-work drink tonight," Carlina continues. "We can go to the kombucheria down the street and you can sample, like, seven kinds. Plus, they're gluten free!"

"I, uh—" I don't know how to process this wave of workplace camaraderie. At my last two jobs, I worked remotely, so I only ever met my coworkers at awkwardly stiff quarterly luncheons or booze-soaked holiday parties. My friendship circle was small before COVID and has dwindled to Gemma and Deondra, the volunteer coordinator at the animal shelter where I volunteer.

Our three computers ping in unison, the sign of a marketing request sent to the general marketing account. Vee sighs and opens up their laptop.

"Captain Fuckface again?" Carlina asks, looking at the bright pink ends of her hair.

"I mean, Captain Fuckface's assistant," Vee replies, their eyes scanning the email. "But I'm sure the missive comes all the way from the top?"

"What is it? And who is Captain, uh, Fuckface?" I ask, opening my computer and trying to remember which combination of childhood pets and numbers I used for a password.

"This is a very urgent marketing request," Carlina explains with the kind of tone that tells me it's anything but. "We get roughly five or so a month, and we're expected to drop everything we're working on just because Captain Fuckface has a brand-new idea he wants to present to the board ASAP."

"And god forbid his royal highness asshole could bear to make a presentation deck on his own," Vee adds. "I bet he's never in his entire life typed up one of his own documents."

"I mean, when Daddy is your venture capitalist and you can claim that you bootstrapped your way to fame, why would you?" Carlina adds.

"It's Callahan, by the way," Vee explains. "Though I'm surprised he hasn't emailed us asking for you specifically." Vee and Carlina make eye contact, and I feel like I'm missing out on a joke.

"How can I help?" I finally unlock my computer and open my email.

"We usually divide and conquer," Vee continues. "One of us handles the copy, the other handles the design. If you can translate this chicken scratch, then you can do the copy." Attached to the email, which just reads *need prez by EOD* is a scan of what looks like a flowchart. The handwriting is difficult to read, but considering I spent a few years working in food expo during college, decoding odd handwriting is a special skill of mine.

"All right," I say, opening a document next to the image. It seems to be a proposal for ConservTech to take over the waste management of smaller, unincorporated areas of Los Angeles county. A note on the side indicates that it would "save taxpayer dollars" and "expedite the county's goals of reaching a net zero waste." A few days ago, I would have jumped at the chance to see Aron's writing and get a glimpse into his mind. But as I begin to sort out his scribbles, I realize that, at best, this idea is half-baked. There's no explanation as to how ConservTech will help the county or where the waste will go. And there's a line at the bottom that says *no union labor?* Checking to see if Vee and Carlina are occupied—they've both opened up a shared illustrator file and are busy inputting the text I'm sending them into the design and they both have headphones on—I take out my phone, make sure the tiny lens is focused, and snap a picture of the flowchart. I zoom in and grab a few details that are hard to see in the original photo.

And then I remember the number I have in my phone.

"I'm hitting the bathroom," I say to Carlina and Vee. Which is weird, right? I'm in my thirties, not in third grade. I don't need permission to pee. But Carlina grunts at her screen and Vee asks me to bring them a coffee back, so it seems like I've flown under the radar. Maybe I should have responded to that CIA recruiter who reached out on LinkedIn...

Deciding to try to be, well, *stealth*, I take the stairs down the twelve floors to the lobby, momentum and a bit of adrenaline guiding my feet as I patter quickly down. Giving a wave to the doorman, I step out onto the sidewalk. I slide on my headphones and click the noise-canceling feature on. I'm weirdly nostalgic for a pay phone booth right now.

I make sure the alley next to the building is empty and duck in. I type in the digits and press Call. The phone rings, and an uncomfortable sense of anxiety takes residence in my bones. I love all the food apps on my phone and the ability to purchase tickets to anything without talking to a human. I *hate* talking on the phone even when there is a goal in mind. But this? As I hear electronic ringing, I rack my brain. How do I introduce myself? Do I say exactly what I'm calling about? Why would he believe me? I can just lie and say it's a wrong number or—

"Hello, Max speaking." A voice answers and breaks me out of my failure to plan.

"Hello?" Like I'm the one answering the call, not the one calling. *Get it together, Brooklyn.*

"Hello, who's calling?"

"Hi, uh, Max. My name is Brooklyn Peters. You were at my apartment last night? Your cousin or sister dated my roommate Gemma? Anyway, it doesn't really matter, because what does matter is that I got your number and I'm curious if we could meet because I think I have something from my new job that might be helpful to some stories that you've worked on in the past?"

He cuts me off quickly. "Are you calling from your office phone?"

"No, I don't even know if I have an office phone—"

"Are you in the office?"

"No, I'm outside. I can go inside if it's loud—"

He lets out a heavy sigh. I can't tell whether it's frustrated or relieved. "No. You're good. Just, uh, don't say anything else on the phone." I hear scrambling. It reminds me of when my mom would look for a pen and a notepad to take down the number of one of my sisters' dates. "What was your name again?"

"Brooklyn. Brooklyn Peters." The sound of pages flipping.

"Okay. Are you free this Sunday? Around ten?"

I do a mental scan of my schedule and realize that I have a whole lot of nothing. "Yeah. I'm free."

"Can you meet me at Norm's in WeHo?"

"Sure. Can you text me the address?"

"Just write it down." Another exasperated sigh. I don't write it down, but I do pull my phone away from my ear and text myself the name of the diner.

"Bring everything you've got," Max is saying. "I'll be wearing a blue shirt and silver glasses." I vaguely wonder if he has any other outfit. "Brooklyn?"

"Yep, sounds great."

"Keep your eyes open." I don't even get a chance to say goodbye or thank you before the line goes dead.

I think that went well? I take the elevator back to the marketing office, and for once, it's blissfully empty of Aron Callahan. Just me and my thoughts and a phone in my pocket with pictures that might be something.

"Where is my coffee?" Vee asks, playing at being offended. I forgot that I was supposed to get them one, and I forgot to pee while I was on my secret mission. Which sucks, because now I actually have to pee. Vee gives me a smile, the glitter of their eyeliner winking under the fluorescent light. "You just owe me a kombucha tonight." And just like that, I'm joining coworkers for drinks after work. Carlina tells me to keep my car in the parking garage for as long as I can, that if we're going to pay "that fucking much," then we deserve every extra minute.

The kombucha is mostly horrible, though there's a lavender one that isn't bad. I settle for drinking an overpriced seltzer in a glass bottle, and Carlina, Vee, and I meander our way through a conversation that is partially getting to know each other and partially shocked that we agree to pay this much for unflavored carbonated water. Carlina walks to her boyfriend's waiting car so he can take her back to K-Town while Vee grabs a rideshare to take them to their apartment on the edge of Hollywood. I walk back to the office building, laughing at a joke Vee made about the NYC subway brand guidelines ("Helvetica? *Groundbreaking.*")

I find a note on my windshield in messy cursive that says:

You're welcome. This was cheaper than buying you lunch. - A

I blush, but I can't tell whether it's from grabbing Aron's attention or whether it's embarrassment. I don't know what he's referring to. Turning on the heat in my car, I drive to the garage attendant, who waves away my ticket and credit card, telling me my parking for the week has been comped.

I think I'm supposed to be flattered, but I'm more confused than anything else. I turn my music up and let the combination of honks of rush-hour traffic and the app-generated playlist streaming through my speakers drown out my thoughts.

Chapter 6

I spend the majority of the rest of the week freaking out every time I get an email, worried it will be Aron following through with the meeting to "check in" on my first week. I was only able to breathe when the gossip around the coffee machine surrounded his trip out of the country to meet with foreign investors. It's not lost on me that he's taking a private company jet.

The minute my nerves about Aron are gone, my nerves about the diner date with Max sneak in. At least seven times on Friday evening, while I'm at happy hour with Carlina and Vee and a few people from other departments, I think about texting him and canceling. But I don't.

Because *what if?*

Sunday morning rolls around and, of course, by the time I get downtown I'm running fifteen minutes late. From there, it takes another ten to find parking. I shot Max a text saying that I would be late, but all I got was a response that said "Noted. Please don't text and drive."

After narrowly missing the car behind me as I parallel park, I breathe a sigh of relief. I tap my phone to pay the meter and notice a text message.

Max: I'm here. I have a table.

I vaguely remember what he looks like, plus I did a cursory google search while waiting for my spin class on Saturday morning. I found his feed for the social media platform formerly known as Twitter and his LinkedIn profile, along with a website featuring a substantial portfolio. The diner is easy to find with its iconic signage, and the door chimes as I walk in. The hostess gives me a thousand-watt smile. "For one?" she asks, and her hair shimmers, I swear. Goddamn LA.

"I'm meeting someone," I respond, looking past her for the real-life version of the staff photos I saw online. I don't know what I expected from someone whose bio includes the hashtag #printsnotdead, but if I had to sketch them, they'd be the guy that was in my kitchen collecting a sweatshirt.

Max, I remind myself. *His name is Max*.

He's wearing a light blue button-up, like he said, with his sleeves rolled to show his forearms. If I had to hazard a guess, I'd put money on the fact he's wearing khakis (khakis!). He's got dark hair that curls in a thousand different directions and tumbles over his forehead, almost covering the tops of his round wire-rimmed glasses. He also mentioned the glasses, though I imagine they'd fit better on the face of a physicist.

But the striking thing about him—well, another striking thing—is that he's reading a *newspaper*. Not the News app on his phone, and not a TikTok video featuring a hipster wearing a beanie, but an honest-to-god *newspaper*. Everyone else here who is solo has their head down over a phone or is tapping at a keyboard, but I'm here to meet with the guy who's reading a newspaper.

Max. His name is Max.

I tell the hostess that I see who I'm meeting and make my way through the Naugahyde booths. I'm happy that I wore leggings, because my legs would stick to these in about seven seconds, even if it is November. The closer I get, the more panic starts to set in. What the fuck am I even doing here? He's going to take one look at these photos and think I'm ridiculous.

"Brooklyn?" Max has noticed me. He puts his newspaper down to the side, folding it like the dad in a Nick at Nite show.

He stands up and holds his hand out, and the difference between us is obvious. He's dressed like a professional, but I'm in leggings and an oversized sweatshirt with the name of the city of the last vacation I took. "Brooklyn Peters?" he repeats.

"That's me," I say, smiling and shaking his hand. It's smooth. I resist the urge to do something to diffuse the tension. Jazz hands maybe. A box step. Everyone loves a good box step.

"Max?" I ask in return. "Max, uh...Matu-sha—." I peter out at the end. When I first got his contact info, I was convinced that his last name was spelled incorrectly.

"Matuschansky," he says, his mouth handling the syllables with ease.

"So that's how you say it," I say, sliding into the booth.

"I think originally there were supposed to be even more vowels, but it turns out, when your family is escaping both the Nazis and then the Soviets, you don't show up with enough money to buy a vowel." He says that sentence with such seriousness that I'm struck dumb for a moment. "Er, sorry," he adds. "Dry humor is how my branch of Jews survived for so long."

"Oh," I say, because I don't know if I'm supposed to laugh or be offended, or if this is some wokeness test. "Anyway, I'm sorry I'm late."

"Sorry to make you drive across the city," he says, sipping a cup of coffee.

"It's nothing." I wave a hand and adopt my mom's midwestern attitude. "You always have to drive somewhere in this city."

"So what made you choose to live in Culver City?" he asks.

I'm all of a sudden worried that this is the beginning of the interview portion of the breakfast. "It was cheap and I needed a roommate. Where do you live?"

"Downtown. Did you grow up here?"

"In the Valley." I pick up the menu. "You?" I'm impressed I can manage small talk.

"Indiana until high school, then Pacific Palisades," he says offhandedly, perusing the menu.

"Oh, someone's fancy," I joke, trying to break this awkwardness.

"Nah, just Jewish," he shoots back quickly. I'm struck again with the feeling that I don't know what I'm supposed to say. The fact of the matter is that Pacific Palisades *is* predominantly Jewish—I know that from reading *LA Times* articles—but I've heard it characterized that way during backyard barbecues out in the Valley, and the tone of those people never made it sound like a positive.

I look down at my own laminated menu while Max asks me a few more questions and we stumble our way into small talk. My coffee arrives, along with the tiny bowl of creamer shots, and I add two to my coffee quickly.

"You know, I love diner mugs," I say before I can think twice. *What a stupid thing to say.*

"Mmm?" Max hums, clearly waiting for me to say more.

"I mean—" I pick mine up and make a show of weighing it in my hands. "They're sturdy. Meant to last a lifetime. Not like the ridiculous mugs you find at the coffee shops in the hipster neighborhoods or in Culver City, right? Those mugs are meant for social media. These mugs are the workhorses of the diner world. Imagine all the grumpy old Angelenos who have sipped coffee from these." I take a healthy sip to underline the point, burning the roof of my mouth in the process.

He gives me a half smile. "You're funny." I can't tell if it's a compliment. We order, and Max continues the conversation.

"Do you have a preference of utensil?" he asks, holding up the rolled silverware, the paper wrapper snugly taped around the collection.

"I rolled so much silverware in my service industry days in college that if I never see another butter knife, I'll die a happy woman."

Max sips his coffee, raises his eyebrows. "What kind of service jobs did you do? Hostess? Waitress?"

I narrow my eyes. "What's with all the questions?"

He rolls his eyes and sighs. "Sorry, it's a journalist thing. Get the subject talking about themselves, and it tends to make everyone more comfortable."

"Subject? I'm not the subject of a scientific study."

He grunts and runs a hand over his face. "No, you're not a subject. If anything, you're a source—"

I pull another face.

"Ugh," he says. "I'm not doing this right." He looks up at the ceiling and murmurs something that sounds like *oy vey*.

"You're not recording this conversation, right?" I have the distinct urge to rip open his shirt to see if he's wearing a wire, but a) that would be weird as fuck, and b) I'm sure technology has advanced since then. "Don't you have to get my permission to record me?"

"No!" Max looks offended. "Though, just so you know—you can't record someone in California without telling them. This is what's called a two-party consent state—"

"I think two-party consent is always a good call," I joke, then clamp my mouth shut when I realize that I've made a sex joke to someone who is supposed to help me out.

It takes a few moments for the joke to register with Max, and when it does, he turns an adorable shade of crimson. "Ah, well, yes. That's a good call, too." We're saved by the waitress dropping off our food—chilaquiles for him, and two eggs, toast, and bacon for me. "Sorry, my mom says the reason I can't find a date is because I never turn the journalism thing off."

I raise my eyebrows and purse my lips. Take a sip of my coffee. Max does the same. I take our strained silence to study him. He looks like he's thinking as he studies his mug. *He's cute*. I haven't dated a lot since lockdown, but back when I used to go out and could handle more than two drinks in an evening, aloof guys like him were the ones I'd ask out after bolstering myself with a little liquid courage.

He taps a finger against the rim of his coffee mug, and I notice he's got long fingers. Nice hands. He clears his throat, and I look up to find him looking at me intently.

"So," I say, dipping a piece of toast into the yolk.

"So," he parrots. I shoot him a look. "Can I see the photos?"

Holding the piece of toast between my teeth, I lean to the side and pull my phone out of the side pocket of my leggings. I do a few swipes to find the photos and make sure to delete a too-sexy one I took last night after two glasses of wine. "Here." I pass the phone across the table.

"Am I okay to swipe through?" He holds up the phone and mimics swiping the screen with his pointer finger. "Nothing, you know, erm, I shouldn't see?" He's that same shade of crimson again.

"No," I say, pretending to act offended, as if I didn't just delete one that featured a sheer bra I bought from an Instagram ad. "Do you think there's actually something there?"

He looks up from where he's zoomed into the series of photos I took of my computer screen and adjusts his glasses. I feel like a professor is about to lecture me. "I'm a journalist who specializes in stories about major corporations skirting environmental law. There's *always* something with these guys. Usually it comes down to messing around with tax law."

"Tax law, huh?" I say, nibbling on a piece of bacon. "Riveting."

"Took down Al Capone."

"Anyone else?"

"Martha Stewart."

"That was insider trading. Plus, she became friends with Snoop and was on the cover of *Sports Illustrated*. In fact, I would argue that going to prison was the best thing that could have happened for her career."

He gives me that same half smile. One could almost call it a smirk. "All these assholes have it coming, though," he says, more to the phone than me.

"On that, we agree." He holds out my phone to me and asks me questions about the flowchart and how I obtained the photo. Cringing at the burn from my second cup of the acid that passes for coffee here, I take a chance.

"So, I did a lot of research for my interview at ConservTech and I, well—" I feel my cheeks heat—"I've followed Aron Callahan's career since undergrad. They've made their biggest acquisitions in waste management throughout the pandemic and beyond. Could it be that they're charging these communities more than the actual cost of the service and pocketing the rest?" Something I came up with last night when I struggled to sleep.

Max brings a pen to his mouth and chews on the cap. The teeth marks that were already there tell me that it's not the first time he's done it. "I mean, it's not outside the realm of possibility." He scribbles a note to himself and runs a hand through his hair, mussing it up a bit more.

I want to mess it up.

He looks up. "Why have you idealized Aron?"

"Huh? I mean, I don't. Well, not anymore." Max raises an eyebrow, and I continue. "Okay, I mean, yeah. I had like, a professional crush on him, but then, well, he's kind of a creep in person? That, combined with this"—I point my fork at my phone—" has kind of dulled the shine."

"It took you two days to see what the vast majority of people refuse to believe. You are full of surprises, Brooklyn Peters." He picks up a chip and munches on it thoughtfully. "Do you think you could get another meeting with Callahan?"

"I mean, probably," I hedge.

"When you see that chance, go for it. See if you can find out more."

"I guess..."

"Brooklyn." Max reaches across the table and takes both my hands in his. There's nothing romantic about this move—it's more of a dramatic appeal—but something zings through me. I realize that it's been so long since I've been touched like this. I make a mental note to get back on the apps this week. "Brooklyn," Max repeats. "There could be something here." His hazel eyes start to shine a bit. I'm almost uncomfortable with his earnestness here, a pure emotion I experienced when I was younger. It's one I pushed down to progress through the corporate world. A hint of a connection.

"Okay," I say, nodding. "Okay. The next time I get invited to the CEO's office, I'll go."

And just like that, I'm living my *Harriet the Spy* fantasy.

Chapter 7

I DO MY BEST to keep my head down over the next few days. I try to blend in and be normal, which is hard, because I don't even know what normal is at a new job. Not when the CEO was making a pass at me on day one and the entire company's mission is a lie.

I've spent most evenings wallowing with Gemma, where she gives me the stink eye and tells me that I shouldn't have trusted any type of corporation because they're all evil. When I point out to her that she is technically trying to get work with evil studios that milk intellectual property until it's dry, she responds by telling me she knew that going into it. Like that makes it any better.

I'm sure if you scratched the surface of my mind, I would have known this at a fundamental level. But after having to give up my dream of swimming with sea turtles for creating marketing materials in a cubicle, I wanted to believe that I could make the world a better place. I recycle. I bring my own bags to the grocery store. I avoid plastic as much as I can. It all feels like the smallest bit of effort against this inevitable gloom of what's coming. A friend of mine from undergrad who ended up working in environmental education said the most difficult part of teaching kids about climate change is figuring out how to do it without sounding like there's nothing they can do and it's all a lost cause.

I never want to accept that it's a lost cause. Silver linings and all that.

I'm not really thinking about that on Thursday. I'm mostly focused on trying to get these two damn images to align on a pamphlet we're putting together for some conference where ConservTech is going to try to convince more local governments to allow them to handle recycling or compost or something that I now know is bullshit.

"It's good enough," Vee says, looking over my shoulder.

"I want it to be perfect," I respond, moving the image over a pixel. My hand slips, and it moves too far. I swear.

"Why? This is just a corporate job," Vee replies. "I'm here to make money so I can do my design work on the side. Carlina's here until she gets her video production company off the ground."

"Well, this is all I've got right now," I say, gritting my teeth. Should I be trying to have a side hustle? It's LA—everyone has their fingers in about a dozen different pies, but it's too much. I guess I'm just simple. I go to work, I hang out with my roommate, I read, and I watch shitty reality television. I used to have more friends, and I used to go on dates, but when everything shut down, it was easy to swaddle myself in my apartment. And I think I've stayed there. It's cozy. And safe.

Carlina lets out a huff of disbelief from her workstation, and I remember that I do have something else. The story with Max, even though I haven't been able to get any more information to confirm my suspicions since I've been trying to be a Good Employee. As if the universe is trying to give me a nudge in the right direction, a notification pops up on the instant messaging app we're forced to use to talk to each other.

AronCallahanCEO: How are you settling in?

BrooklynPetersMarketing: Just fine.

BrooklynPetersMarketing: I really enjoy working here.

AronCallahanCEO: Excellent.

AronCallahanCEO: I would love to hear more about how your first weeks have been.

I know it's not a request, but a demand, like a new employee can "decline" an invitation from the CEO of the entire damn company. A thought flits through my brain, and I wonder if I'm the first new female employee he's invited up to his office, but I push it away. Maybe he really is just trying to ensure that I'm settling in here. I quickly click *accept* on the invite, which is for a meeting in his office at four this afternoon.

I reach for my phone and swipe quickly, letting Gemma know what's going on, to which she responds with *OMG* and a frantic series of questions that I don't have time to respond to. I go back to the marketing pamphlet, only stopping to break for a quick lunch in the cafeteria. I wrap up the project at quarter to four and answer emails for the next fifteen minutes, then I gather my things.

"Leaving early, Staten Island?" Carlina asks, looking up from her computer and pulling out an earbud.

"I have a meeting," I say, hoping she doesn't ask any further questions.

"With?" Vee pries.

"Aron, uh, Mr. Callahan," I stammer.

Carlina and Vee share a knowing look.

"What's that?" I ask, waving a hand between them.

"You're his new favorite," Carlina says in a way that lets me know it's not a good thing.

"What does that mean?"

"It means that about once a quarter, a new hot young thing gets hired, and all of a sudden, the CEO gets *very* interested in the 'worker's experience,'" Vee explains.

"And?" I ask, nervous to see where this sentence goes.

"And usually a few months later, she quits with a fat settlement and a signed NDA," Carlina adds. "Or at least, that's what we think."

Add another thing to the list of how ConservTech has let me down. Aron Callahan has gotten awards from notable feminist and queer advocacy organizations for being an ally and for his donations. The company, allegedly, has incredibly inclusive policies. So not only do I need to try to find examples of their environmental misdeeds, but I need to protect myself from sexual harassment.

Great.

All of these thoughts are spinning through my head as I follow through the maze of hallways to his office suite. Instead of looking at me skeptically, the secretary is expecting me this time.

"Ms. Peters," she says and gives me a knowing smile that makes my stomach turn. Aren't women supposed to support other women? There's a not-insignificant part of me that feels like I'm walking into the lion's den. She leads me down the hallway to Aron's office suite and opens the door without knocking. It looks the same as the first time I was here, but it's more ominous somehow, with a new light shed on everything after my meeting with Max and what Vee and Carlina just told me.

Aron enters from a second room—an antechamber?—and gives me a sly smile. "Ms. Peters, so good to see you." I smile back, even though I feel a chill run down my spine. He looks past me and sees the secretary waiting. "That will be all, Brenda. Have a great day." He dismisses her with a nod, and she closes the door behind her.

"Sit, sit, Brooklyn," he says, indicating one of the leather chairs across from his desk. When he settles in behind the desk, I'm grateful for the slab of wood between us, a barrier that feels like it could be my only protection at the moment. He leans over and pulls out a bottle of brown liquid from a desk drawer and two glasses. Without asking, he pours two fingers into each and slides one across the desk to me.

I take a moment to study him. Aron *is* attractive. He's got the type of face that comes from generations of wealth, a lack of hard work, and the assumption that everything is going to go his way. His jaw is sharp, and there is a suspicious lack of smile lines around his eyes and mouth. Maybe due to Botox, though I've never seen him smile, so I can't rule that out. Sure, he smirks, but it's not the same. I suppose, in a different life, I'd be flattered by his attention. Maybe straight-out-of-college Brooklyn would have thought she was special, thought that she could bring a smile to his stern mouth.

Unbidden, an image of Max's face flashes in my head. He wasn't warm during our meeting, but he was honest. Optimistic. In the time since, he's been terse and efficient in the few text messages we've sent back and forth with simple updates on how I haven't been able to find anything. But hopefully I get to send him something else this evening.

I shove that image down and focus on the task at hand, which is making sure I have an exit strategy.

Aron is asking questions about how I'm enjoying work and why I chose to work here, and I'm answering, but my heart isn't in it.

Focus, Brooklyn. Eyes on the prize. Other things your high school coaches told you that you didn't pay attention to.

"Aron?" I ask, interrupting him and resisting the urge to cringe. "Can I ask you a question?" Feeling all sorts of icky, I lean forward just a bit, allow my blouse to gap a millimeter.

"Yes?" He smirks, one corner of his mouth kicking up.

CORPORATE MANDATED HOLIDAY ROMANCE 45

I release a breathy sigh, hating myself a bit, and continue. "What's the newest plan? I mean, I saw the email you sent, and I was curious."

"You don't need to worry about any of that." He laughs, and I feel like he just patted me on the head and told me to go get ice cream.

"I want to learn, though." I push a bit further and try for flattery. "I've followed your career, and I've always admired your mind."

"I'd rather you admire other things of mine," he says, sex slipping into his voice.

"I'm just saying that there is something about the way the business works that—"

"No, Brooklyn." His voice is sharp, the same one he used on day one with his secretary, the one I've heard barking through the phone at Carlina. "I don't share how things work with anyone, and I certainly don't share it with you. Do you really think I brought you up here to talk about business strategy?" He snorts. "Brooklyn, someone in HR hired you, and you've caught my attention, but it's certainly not for your business acumen."

"I, uh," I stammer.

"Go back to your office, Brooklyn. And come back when you've grown up." I leave with my tail between my legs. I get back to the office, which is mercifully empty of Carlina and Vee and their questioning glances, and flop into my chair, my head in my hands. My phone buzzes. It's Max confirming our plans for breakfast again this Sunday. I send a pathetic thumbs-up. I don't like not being good at things. It's why I've stayed in my lane. I don't like the beginning stages of doing a new job, so I've continued taking jobs that I know I can do. I hate the awkwardness of first dates and feeling like I didn't do a good enough job for a second one. Shit, I stopped going to therapy when I realized that I just had to do it forever.

I want people to like me, which is probably why I haven't started a lot of friendships. That would be something to bring up to my therapist if I was still in therapy. So I don't like that I messed up with Aron today. I don't like that I have to tell Max that I failed, and I don't like that Carlina and Vee view me as someone who is trying to suck up to Captain Fuckface.

I text Gemma a plea to order emergency Thai food again tonight.

Chapter 8

That weekend, I'm late to the diner again, and again, Max is sitting there, reading the *LA Times* and drinking a cup of coffee. He looks like he did the last time I was here, though I was filled with excitement and hope then. Now, I'm just depressed, and I feel like I'm on my way to tell my teacher that I didn't do my homework.

"Hi," I say, tapping on the back of his newspaper. He puts it down and gives me a stern look, like *excuse me, I was learning about water restrictions*. Which he probably was, because it's California.

"Hello," he replies, folding the newspaper. Everything that happened on Friday spills out of me in a clunky avalanche of words, even though I spent all of Saturday planning what to say. With every sentence, I watch Max's reactions. He begins by pinching the bridge of his nose. Then he takes off his glasses. Next, he puts his glasses back on, messing his hair in the process. By the end of my explanation, he has the look of a parent who had to corral ten seven-year-olds to get to the Disney Christmas parade.

Max runs his hands through his air, tugging a bit and pulling it out to a length that is beginning to look absurd. "There has to be a way for me to get in there."

"Don't you trust me? As a source?" I know I'm not a journalist, but I'm a millennial, so I do know how to find someone on social media and how to stealthily snap a photograph of a hot guy from across the bar to send to a friend.

"No, that's not quite it," Max says stiffly. "Brooklyn, you've got great instincts—look at what you've gotten so far. However, the more eyes on this, the better. You never want to rely on just one perspective." Max takes his glasses off and polishes them on his shirt. "Any job openings?"

"Not that I know of," I respond. "Plus, the hiring cycle is like seven months if you're fast tracked. By the time I got my job offer, I had basically forgotten that I even interviewed." A year of cover letters and four rounds of interviews seemed worth it when I was chasing my dream job. My, how times have changed.

"Great point," he says begrudgingly. There's something about Max that makes me think he's never satisfied and is always searching for a better answer or a quicker solution. My brain quickly jumps to wondering if he's ever satisfied in bed.

Why? Why does my brain do this?

To distract myself, I start processing my thoughts out loud. "It's annoying, because there are all of these bizarre team-building socialization events." Max looks over the rims of his glasses at me and motions for me to continue. "They're technically not required, but there's the assumption that if you don't go, then you're not being a good employee and that you don't have fun."

"Corporate mandated fun time," he says warily.

"Exactly." I roll my eyes. "They're mostly at the office, because apparently, we don't spend enough time there." I'm starting to realize how much I already dislike working at ConservTech. Crap, now I'm already dreading the idea of applying for jobs again. Especially if what I think I saw on those documents is accurate and if Max and I can break this story. But then I think about Vee and Carlina. They've gotten me out of the house more than anyone in the past few years. Since I met them, I even say hi to people outside my department around the coffee machine. I even know their names.

"Do they let other people join these events?" Max asks, scribbling a note on the corner of a napkin.

"Not just anyone, but significant others are invited to most of the events."

"That's it!" Max slaps the pencil down on the table.

"But I'm single? And you don't work there, so you can't bring a girlfriend. Or boyfriend."

"Brooklyn, I can go as your boyfriend."

"We're not dating?" I'm assaulted by images of what it would be like to spend the vast majority of my time with Max. Of how he would have to get the newspaper every morning and read it while drinking black coffee at his dining room table.

I would bet he knows all the paper delivery people by name.

"*Brooklyn,*" Max sighs, saying my name in the manner that one would speak to a dog who was struggling with a new trick. "We wouldn't really be dating. I'd pretend to be your boyfriend so I could get into the office."

It's not a rejection at all, but it still stings like one.

"This is a perfect plan," Max continues, flipping open his notebook and beginning to make notes on the page. "You can dazzle everyone with your good looks and jokes, and while they're distracted, I can slip into offices and recycling bins." Max's eyes are bright as he imagines what it could be like to reassemble shredded documents, but my brain is still stuck on what he said.

Good looks and jokes.

"Okay, I can't tell if you're serious."

"I'm always serious," Max says seriously.

"Okay, well, don't kid about my looks in all of this."

"What?"

"Or my sad jokes."

Max takes his glasses off. "Those are just objective truths. You're beautiful and you're funny. It makes sense that you would be the center of attention."

"Oh."

"And going undercover is a classic journalistic technique. It's hard to do now with social media, so this is selfishly a chance for me to break a huge story and go undercover."

"Okay," I say, slightly chastised and oddly flattered.

"Fun fact: we're following in the footsteps of one of my favorite journalists, who got herself committed to an asylum in the 1900s to expose their inhumane mental health practices."

"Did you just compare the company I work for to a turn-of-the-century asylum?"

Max grins, then takes a sip of the coffee that has definitely grown cold. "If the shoe fits." I toss my paper napkin ring at him. It bounces off his nose, and he barely flinches. He's all business now, his pencil dancing across the page of his notebook. "When's the next one?"

I pull out my phone and open my work calendar, tap until I get to the ConservTech Team Fun! Calendar. The month is awash with dates in red and green. "There are like twenty to choose from." I turn my phone screen toward him, and he pinches and zooms and investigates.

"These are all Christmas parties." His voice is flat.

"They're holiday parties."

That Max glare again. "Everything is red and green. There's a reindeer on the email. I'm pretty sure that other religions don't decorate using small multicolored lights. I've never heard of a Diwali ungulate or a Kwanzaa sled."

"Okay?"

"Here's the thing. I don't *do* Christmas. I'm Jewish, remember? I do my best to hibernate throughout the month of December, only to emerge to see a movie and eat Chinese food on the twenty-fifth."

"I mean, it's not a big deal," I say. The minute the words are out of my mouth, I know it's the wrong thing to say. I've said stupid things around Max before—hell, I think most of what I say around Max is stupid—but this elucidates a different look.

"No, Brooklyn." I have an uncomfortable flashback to when I fucked up my attempt at solo investigation with Aron. "This is not the same thing as when some guy complains on the *Jeopardy* Facebook page that the final question was about the Kardashians. I ignore Christmas because it's a way of self-preservation."

"You follow the *Jeopardy* Facebook page?"

"Not the point. Have you ever lived through an entire month where everything around you reminds you of the fact that you don't belong? That the calendar and holidays aren't yours? Do you know what year COVID happened in the Jewish calendar?"

"Well, time is a flat circle," I attempt to joke, but Max gives a frustrated sigh.

"It occurred in the year 5781. The Mayan calendar gets more press than the Jewish calendar does."

"It says they're just holiday events?" I can already tell I'm flailing.

"When I was in middle school in Indiana, my parents took us out of school for the High Holidays. They were unexcused absences. My parents got a letter from the Indiana State Board of Education with a warning that I was in danger of being truant for the year. For my religious observances."

"I'm sorry," I say softly.

"You didn't do it."

"Still feels like something I'm supposed to say here?"

Max gives a dry laugh. "It's better than a lot of the responses I've received. Usually people tell me to get over it."

"That's stupid."

"Well, you listened."

"Just another reason you should fake date me at the Corporate Mandated Holiday Fun Time." I dump an extra creamer in my coffee and give him a big, corny smile.

"I'm not doing Christmas things," he says. "Plus, I don't really know Christmas things. I know there's a man who sneaks down your chimney." He pumps his eyebrows once, underlining the innuendo. I let out a giggle and get another idea.

"I can train you! My parents are divorced, and my mom loves the holiday, so Christmas was a big ordeal when I was growing up. I'll teach you the right songs and jokes and all the warm and fuzzy cultural stuff."

"Warm and fuzzy like the man who weirdly knows where every child in the world lives?" Max's wry humor is back, so I can tell he's warming up to the idea.

"I'll even let you in on the secret that the Santa we all imagine is based on a Coca-Cola advertisement. How's that for corporate evil-doing?"

He lets out a huff, and I feel like it's a victory to get him to laugh.

Point, Brooklyn.

"I feel like I need to get you a disguise."

"We'll stick close to the truth. We met through your roommate, who used to date my sister. I can say I do something vague and boring that no one cares about—I'll say I work in finance." He pulls a face.

"How is your sister?" I ask out of politeness.

"She took the breakup pretty roughly but has a great job bartending in Colorado now." Max says. "Could be worse. My grandmother locked my grandfather in a fruit cellar and escaped to America to start over because he wouldn't grant her a divorce."

"You're joking."

"Brooklyn, I've never lied to you." He puts his hand over his chest.

"Scout's honor?"

"The Boy Scouts are antisemitic *and* homophobic," is his reply.

"That's...not surprising," I say. "Okay, so Max Matuschan—" I let my attempt at his last name stick in my throat, like my courage. "You are now my boyfriend."

"Mazel tov on the beginning of our new relationship."

"Well, at least you get a cool backstory. I guess I'm stuck being the girl who didn't get to save the rainforest or be a marine biologist but mostly spends her time formatting Instagram posts and correcting grammar for PR releases." Sometimes—well, most times when Gemma is out at an event and the apartment is empty—I think about how boring my life is. How I settled at every turn. Nothing is actually horrible in my life, comparatively. I can put food on the table and a roof above my head, but it doesn't feel *vibrant*.

And maybe that's why I snapped those photos after I realized that ConservTech was just another company in a line of companies. Maybe I wanted to bring a little adventure into my life. I remember myself as a little girl, Lisa Frank notebook in hand, with elaborate plans to become Eliza Thornberry. Travel the world, save animals. I would lose sleep thinking about acid rain and the hole in the ozone layer. But at some point, there became too many news stories to follow. A constant stream of white noise about a failing planet and apathetic populace.

And I did what everyone else did, too.

I tuned out.

And here is Max, offering to add a bit of spark to my life.

"Let's do it." I reach my hand across the table. Max does too, and we shake on it.

"What does *mazel tov* mean?" I say, trying to hit the syllables like Max did.

"Good luck. Something we'll need a lot of."

Just like that, I'm an undercover journalist. And I have a boyfriend.

Mazel tov, indeed.

Chapter 9

Max and I decided that a few things needed to happen before he just showed up at a work event.

I had to drop the fact that I was dating someone often enough that it would be weird if I didn't bring him.

Max had to pick me up from work a few times so people would know what he looks like.

We had to text regularly during the workday so his name would pop up on my phone.

We swapped phones to take selfies and update contact information with addresses and last names. When I got mine back to see how he had added his last name (I still had to double check the spelling), I rolled my eyes and gave an exasperated sigh.

"What?" Max said.

"It just says your first name and your last name."

"So?"

"Look at mine," I command, and a few taps and swipes of Max's finger bring up my name, which I've entered as:

🏙️ Brooklyn💜

"It's cute because, like, I'm named after a city, and then the hearts. Because we are desperately, madly in love."

"I don't think this is the New York skyline," Max says, sliding his glasses down his nose and looking closely at the phone. "Plus, is anyone madly in love in Los Angeles? Most people I know have hookups they tolerate."

"That is so pessimistic," I say automatically. "Just because you've seen nothing but bad examples, that doesn't mean there isn't the possibility of something better in the future. I mean, my parents got divorced when I was eight, and I still think that true love is possible."

"Hence why you're single?" Max is in journalism mode, so I shut that down quickly.

"Not now, reporter. Back to emojis."

"Why did you do this?" Max says, grimacing. "Emojis are for children."

I scoff. "Emojis are a representation of a millennia-long history of pictorial graphics!" He looks chastened for a second, so I add, "Plus, they're cute. And if we were actually dating, we'd probably have our names in our phones with emojis."

"We're in our thirties, Brooklyn."

"Bah, growing up is boring," I respond. I chew on my lower lip as I decide which emoji to add to his name.

"Put a newspaper," he suggests, scrolling through the options on his own phone.

"That's too obvious." I continue to chew my lip and rattle off a few suggestions—pencil, his favorite animal, a car. Finally, I decide to suggest something just to get a reaction out of him. I look up from my phone to find that his eyes have glazed over a bit, focusing on something. I probably, quite literally, have egg on my face.

"So an eggplant, then?"

"Huh?"

"Max, focus! This is important!"

He responds by mumbling something about *damn distractions*. "No eggplant. Put a stack of books and a heart."

"What's your favorite color?"

"Blue."

I adjust his name accordingly and look at our message, noticing something I haven't before. "You don't have read receipts on!"

"It seems creepy. And overly invasive."

"We're going *undercover*, unless you've forgotten that."

"Aron and ConservTech deserve to be taken down. No one needs to know if I've seen their invitation for coffee or drinks." I freeze with my cup halfway to my mouth.

"Are there a lot of people asking you out?" Fear hits me. If he's dating someone, it feels super fucked up to ask him to fake date me, especially when I don't know what I'm doing and I'm working on a gut instinct. I don't even trust my gut with too much sriracha or dairy. Why am I trusting it with taking down a Fortune 500 CEO?

"No." Max snorts his answer as if it's a ridiculous thing to even suggest.

"You don't date?" I ask.

"I have dated. I just tend to be really busy, and most people don't want to put up with the unpredictable work schedule of a journalist. Plus, most people I meet aren't Jewish, and for a long time, I didn't think I would ever date a Gentile. But now I'm more open to it, so there's a cultural divide I'm constantly having to explain. On top of that, well"—he adjusts his glasses again—"it takes me a while to warm up to people."

"Are you dating anyone?" Max parrots my question back to me.

"Nada. And before you ask, it's not because I have some repressed childhood trauma or have a moral objection to apps. I like sex, and I like relationships. It's just, well, Los Angeles."

"You've lived here all your life."

"And still haven't found a man in all of the City of Angels that I enjoy."

"Second largest city in the United States," he says, smiling.

"Maybe I should try my shot in New York."

"Fits with your name." He holds up his phone to where my contact information is still up. "And your emojis."

We plan to begin texting the next day at work.

As much as it pains me, I realize that I have to unmute my phone so I can make a big deal about getting a text from my boyfriend. My phone has been on mute since Obama's first term—so long that when a sound pings through the marketing department, I don't even realize it's my phone.

"Manhattan, will you get that?" Carlina has decided to rotate through all five boroughs and New York neighborhoods instead of calling me by my actual name. At first, I was annoyed, but after she called Vee every other letter in the alphabet one week, I realized that it's how she shows love.

"What?"

"Washington Heights, that is your phone. And it's making a *noise*. Which is auditorily offensive." Carlina slips her noise-canceling headphones back on and makes a huge show of plugging them into her computer. Vee and I share a smile as I unlock my phone.

Max: Hello, girlfriend that I regularly text throughout my day.

I let out a bit of a snort-laugh that has Vee curious. "Interesting message?" they ask. And at that moment, I remember something. Something really fucking critical that I should have remembered much earlier.

As much as my dad's girlfriend tried to get me to have a big break as a child actor, putting me in camps and classes in elementary school, there's a reason I gravitated toward science and design. I am a *horrible* actress. My acting skills would make *The Room* look like an Oscar-winner.

"Uh," I stutter. "This was my boyfriend. Is my boyfriend." I hold up my phone and give it a weird little wave. "I will text him back!"

"Okay?" Vee rolls their eyes and looks back down at their iPad.

Brooklyn: Hello, boyfriend that I also text throughout my day.

Brooklyn: And who loves emojis.

Max: They are my favorite.

Brooklyn: So what are you up to today?

There's a pause, and three dots pop up, then retreat, then pop up again, then leave. I put my phone down and roll my eyes.

"I didn't know you had a boyfriend," Vee says, looking up.

"I didn't. I did. I mean, I do." I pinch the bridge of my nose. "His name is Max."

"Sounds cute. How'd you meet?"

My brain goes blank, and I'm saved from having to answer by my phone pinging again.

"Turn that shit off," Vee says.

I open my phone to find something I've never seen before. It's a *paragraph* of emojis. From Max. I don't even try to decode it yet, instead choosing to send a WTF GIF to him. If he hates emojis, I bet he loathes GIFs.

Max: That movie is inaccurate.

Brooklyn: You're right. I totally thought that four idiot white men could get drunk and meet Mike Tyson.

Brooklyn: It was more to convey the WTF for this paragraph.

Max: I am giving your mind something to work on. Plus, it's part of our hilarious and loving backstory.

Brooklyn: You're ridiculous.

Vee clears their throat, and I hastily put my phone away and head back to work on the layout for our next brochure. I find the flow state that I love about designing, considering the ways in which I use native plants to highlight the different areas that our company works in, until I'm interrupted with a knock on the door of the marketing studio.

"Ms. Peters?" That voice, which only a few weeks ago would have sent shivers down between my legs and made my knees go a bit weak, now sends a jolt of fear ricocheting through my body.

"Mr. Callahan. Aron," I say, dropping my stylus and looking up from my tablet.

"There's someone here to see you," he says, raising one eyebrow and looking me up and down, his eyes lingering on my chest. I'm leaning over my workstation, and my loose blouse has gaped open a bit. I hastily cover my chest, with Carlina and Vee watching on with eager, curious eyes.

"Who?" I sputter, standing up.

"Knock, knock, sugarplum," comes Max's voice. He pokes his head out from behind Aron's frame, and I have to suppress a giggle. Seeing them next to each other, the differences are apparent. Aron is broad shoulders and sleek hair, somehow manspreading into the room even as he stands in the doorway. Max is a riot of half-contained curls and glasses, a wry smirk on his face and a furtive look in his eyes that has me wondering how anyone doesn't know that we're up to something.

Aron's body language screams *domination* and *control.*

Max's body language screams *shenanigans*.

And, god help me, I've always been up for shenanigans.

"Max!" I exclaim, wondering if I should have some cutesy term of endearment for him. "What are you doing here?"

"I thought I'd take you out for a surprise lunch."

I know it's fake. I know he's not my boyfriend. I know this was planned so he could understand the layout of the office so it's easier when we're at the event later this week, but still. The idea of someone surprising me for a lunch, even if it's at the food court at the mall down the street, warms my heart.

That's never happened before.

"Is that okay, Aron?" I ask, my eyes flicking from Max to Aron, back and forth. It's unusual for a CEO to bring a visitor, but it's also unusual for a CEO to drop by a department to check up on the work, which Aron has been doing more and more. He has a tendency to lean over my back while I'm working and speak directly into my ear, almost at a whisper level.

"As long as you get your work done," he responds and turns to Max. His voice turns slick and corporate, the same way he reprimanded the office manager on day one. It's different from the low, growly voice he used during our meetings. I note the difference and file it away in my brain to hastily tap out on my Notes app during lunch. "It's always nice to meet the partners of our valued employees. Max...?" He trails off, and Max fills in the blank.

"Matuschansky," he responds, leaning into the accent. I swear I can see the Cyrillic letters spill from his lips.

"Max," Aron repeats, not even giving an attempt at his last name. "Well." And with a nod, Aron turns to leave, but Max, as always, is quick on his feet.

"Can I have a tour? This is my first time I've been here since Brook started." We didn't discuss nicknames, and usually I hate when people give me a nickname without asking, but it's funny coming from Max. A nickname from the man who barely uses contractions in a text message. While my brain is spinning, Max is continuing, laying on the charm about how excited I am to work here and how much he's heard about it. Vee and Carlina have given up any pretense of working. They've set their styluses down and turned their bodies to follow the scene.

I turn back to Aron, ready to apologize or beg or something to keep this from going off the rails. Plus, I'm really hungry and there's a great sandwich shop down the street. Where I expect to see him looking at Max with disdain or annoyance, I'm surprised to find his eyes on me. They've changed since our initial meetings, even from earlier today. He looks predatorial, the same way I've seen in wildlife documentaries when a predator has found the weak member of the herd and is preparing to strike.

"I'd be so happy to show you around," Aron says, his voice sharp. "After all, I am CEO of this company."

"Oh!" Max says, fake surprise in his voice. "I had no idea."

"It'd be wonderful to show you around so you can understand how vital Brooklyn is to this entire operation." Aron looks back at me, and I realize what this all is. I misjudged the animal metaphor. Instead of Aron trying to attack Max, he's puffed up, displayed his bright feathers in the most ridiculous manner possible.

This is the world's worst avian mating dance.

We chuckle about it afterward at lunch. "He's not subtle, is he?" I ask, taking a bite out of the dill pickle that accompanies my sandwich. Max insisted on paying, shushing any argument by explaining that I had to work with that "pompous asshole" every day.

"Not at all." Max laughs into his glass bottle of seltzer. "I mean, basically, he was the Beast telling Belle that there was no way she should ever go to the west wing, and we all know how that ends up."

"What if he knows what we're up to and he thinks that this is a way to lure you into a false sense of comfort? What if he's leaving breadcrumbs to bring us into a trap?" My grip on the sandwich tightens so much the toasted bun crunches.

"Brook, he's not that smart," Max says. "He's just rich and threatened."

"Threatened by what?"

"The fact that he can't have you." Max lifts his eyebrows once. "He was basically peeing over every corner of the office on our tour."

"Oh."

"It's killing him," Max continues. "Because guys like *that* aren't used to being told no, especially when it has to do with women."

"Isn't that sexual harassment and against, like, every labor law and standard in California?"

"And isn't what you took a photo of against every environmental law in this state and country?"

"Okay, fair point."

"Fun fact," he replies, grinning at me. "California environmental law also protects archaeological and historical sites."

I roll my eyes. "Fascinating."

I crumple up my sandwich wrapper while Max nibbles on a dill pickle in a way that is slightly obscene. "Remember, there's an event on Friday. Are you free?"

"Let me clear my schedule for all my interviews with Anderson Cooper," he replies, deadpan. I throw a straw wrapper at him. "Yes, Brook, I'm free. What is it, again?"

Looking at my phone, I take in the overwhelming schedule of "fun" events and settle on what seems like the most innocuous one. Something about bingo, which seems like we don't have to do much talking to anyone else. Right after undergrad, when I started volunteering at the animal shelter, I helped to run the snack bar at the monthly fundraiser bingo game. If I could handle all the grandmas, abuelas, and lolas who rolled in with their massive carriers full of a variety of bingo daubers, then a little corny workplace bingo will be nothing.

Chapter 10

Thirty minutes into the event, I'm thinking that allowing whatever horrible environmental regulatory laws ConservTech is skirting to continue would be preferable to this bingo-slash-icebreaker night.

Max and I got there on time, which meant that we were two of only a handful of people in the large conference space. I grabbed a seltzer, and Max picked up a cranberry juice from the cooler. I applauded myself for not making a UTI joke. Which was irrelevant, because I told Max how proud I was for not making that joke a few seconds later, which he pointed out, was actually worse than telling the joke in the first place. We made awkward conversation with two accountants and an intern from the data analysis project for a few minutes until the smell of clove heralded Vee's arrival.

"Oh, thank god," I breathed, grabbing their arm. "This is the worst?"

"Heh, yeah, Carlina and I only attend these things to see how horrible they are, like how there's been a midnight showing of *The Ring* for the last two decades." Carlina is next, coughing a bit as she comes in, accompanied by the faint odor of cannabis. "Want an edible?" Vee asks Max and me, holding out a tin.

"No, the last time I did one of those, everything turned yellow and I was afraid of my comforter," I respond.

"I'm neurotic enough as it is," Max adds.

"What a pair," Carlina says, her slightly reddened eyes bouncing from Max to me. I realize then, or remember, that we're here as a couple. And couples touch. Usually. Max and I have a solid six inches of space between our bodies, and his arms are crossed. I reach over and gently tug one of his hands out from the crook of his elbow and hold hands with him.

"What are you doing?" he whispers as Carlina and Vee head off to see someone they know in another department.

"I dunno, couple-y things," I hiss back.

"Is this how you hold hands when you're in a couple?" He holds up our hands, which aren't linked together. We're palm to palm, almost swinging our hands between us, more like the Whos in Whoville at the end of *The Grinch* than two people who are in love.

"I mean," I begin, not ready to explain that I haven't held hands with anyone like this in years. With a grunt, Max shifts his fingers and interlaces them with mine. It's an unfamiliar touch; I'm not used to the knobbiness of his knuckles or the way the one ring I'm wearing presses into the side of my finger. We both shift again, and I feel my hands grow damp. "It's fine," I finally say, pulling my hand away and wiping it on my slacks and hoping that the sweat marks don't show.

"Are you comfortable with...?" Max trails off as he places an arm on my low back.

"That's okay," I respond. It's more than okay. It's one of my favorite things former boyfriends and dates have done, but it wouldn't be fair to Max to dump all of that on him. He inches his hand a bit farther so the tips of his fingers are at my hip and tugs me just a little closer.

"See? Couple things." He gives me a grin. "Now who can you introduce me to that will easily spill all the secrets?"

"Hush," I scold, but there's no heat in it. Max and I shuffle, still connected, over to a table where Vee is chatting to a few of their friends who are on the biology team. They make introductions, and I wave, explain that I'm new here, and participate in the vague corporate complaining that is normal for any of us who have to work.

Vee pumps their eyebrows once and sips what looks like a gin and tonic. "Do you know who's taken *special interest* in our dear, sweet designer here?"

"Vee," I warn, but a woman turns to Vee and immediately asks them if they mean what they're saying.

"Did you get a meeting with Captain Fuckface on your first week here?" they ask.

"I don't even think he knows what the biology department is working on," the woman, whose name, I learned, is Micah, says. She turns her amber eyes on me and points a serious finger. "Be careful, Brooklyn. Last year, one of our new biologists caught his attention. She didn't last a month."

"Well," her friend Megan adds. "It didn't help that she started asking all sorts of questions about the budget."

Micah rolls her eyes. "I've made peace with it all. There are certain battles that I'm willing to fight and certain things that I have to let slide. I already have too many gray hairs, and I'm barely forty." She clinks her glass against Megan's bottle of ginger beer.

Megan looks over and gives us a skeptical look. "Hi, I don't believe we've met." She holds her hand out toward Max.

Fuck. I forgot to introduce Max. Which is something that a girlfriend would do. "This is Max!" I jump in, a little too loud.

"What department do you work with?" she asks.

"Oh, no. He's my boyfriend. He works with numbers," I respond, still a few decibels over what a normal conversation should be.

"Doing what?" Micah asks.

"Finance," Max responds.

At the same time, I say, "Accounting."

"Huh?"

"Finance," Max repeats, a little more forcefully.

"What does that even mean?" Vee wonders aloud. "Like, it's like saying that I work in 'photos' when design and marketing encapsulate so much more."

Max is silent, and I can see that he's racking his brain, trying to find something that sounds genuine and honest. "Yeah, but like, do the nuances even matter to anyone outside of our little niche?" I hastily add, trying to deflect.

Vee shrugs. "I guess you're right." We stumble over questions about how we met, earning suspicious looks from Vee, empathetic nods from Megan, and skeptical grunts from Micah. Finally, blessedly, Aron steps to the front of the room. He's wearing his standard black bespoke suit. Every millimeter of fabric molded to his skin, but he has exchanged his typical black tie for a deep crimson one. Festive, I guess.

"Happy Holidays," he says, allowing himself a half smile. "I'm so happy you all have joined for these events. Not only do they help underscore how the ConservTech team is a family, but attendance at these events factors into our raise, bonus, and advancement structure."

"That seems a violation of labor law," Max whispers in my ear, making goose bumps spring up across the back of my neck and down

CORPORATE MANDATED HOLIDAY ROMANCE   69

my chest. "Or, at the very least, ethics." I purse my lips as I look at him. There's a sparkle in his eye, like the old illustrations of Santa. Something that is both kind and warm but with an undertone of shenanigans. It matches the sparkle I'm feeling in my fingers and my toes. I turn to look at Max. We're close. We're *really* close. And I can feel his breath on my cheek—

"I'll pass things over to my secretary, Brenda, who offered to put this event together." Aron speaks over the crowd.

"More like was voluntold," Megan stage whispers to the table.

"I mean, it's bingo. How hard can it be?" I ask. Bingo cards are passed out, and I flip mine over, expecting to see the usual array of number and letter combinations, but this is something different.

"Fuck," Micah says. "My sister is a teacher, and she does this shit with her third graders."

Instead of bingo numbers, it's categories.

Has gone skiing in Vail for Christmas.
Spent more than one day putting up Christmas lights.
Grew up with a white Christmas.
Has dressed up as Santa.
Uses Amazon Prime to wrap their gifts.
Goes caroling.
Has touched a reindeer.
Owns a pickle ornament.
Likes Elf on the Shelf.
Doesn't like Elf on the Shelf.
Believed in Santa until after ten years of age.

"So," Brenda explains, "you'll mingle around the room and find someone who fits each of these categories. They'll sign the box that fits them, and the first employee to black out their bingo cards wins."

"I wish I could black out," Vee says, making their way over to the cash bar.

Max is looking at his bingo card with a disgusted face. It takes me a second to realize why. Every single one of these categories is related to Christmas. Even the ones that are ostensibly about winter are Christmas related. There's nothing about New Year's or non-religious holidays. Hell, there aren't even references to the holidays that aren't Christmas.

"I'm so sorry," I apologize hastily. "I didn't know. I honestly thought that it would just be us crossing off squares like we're a bunch of grandmas."

"First off, if we were, the spirit of my bubbewould be kicking everyone's ass. Second off, it's not your fault, Brooklyn. You didn't make this bingo card." He looks up and eyes Brenda, who is wearing an absolutely absurd red sweater with a fur trim. "What is the Elf on the Shelf?"

"Well, it's this thing that is big with parents who have kids now—it wasn't around when we were kids—it's a stuffed elf who flies down from the North Pole and watches the kids' behavior and reports it to Santa." Max's eyebrows are in danger of disappearing completely into his hair. "And, like, sometimes parents get really into it and set up these elaborate scenarios and then, well, the kids aren't allowed to touch the elf?"

"I'm sorry, what?" Max snorts out a bit of his cranberry and soda. "You're telling me that people do this on purpose? This is nothing but training young children to be comfortable with the constant surveillance that is embedded in new technology. This is like the Patriot Act for children!"

"Yeah, now that I'm saying all of it, it's pretty bonkers." I hold up my bingo card and point to the square that says *Doesn't like Elf on the Shelf*. "But now we know what you can sign?"

Chapter 11

WE STUMBLE THROUGH THE rest of the bingo event with each of us taking a fifteen-minute break in the hallway to avoid awkward conversations. It turns out that everyone is nosy about our relationship—*where did you meet? What do you do?* Blah, blah, blah. Max barely got three minutes to chat with Micah about budgeting conditions before someone else wanted to know about us. I agreed to drive Max home, seeing as I didn't drink and we needed time to process whatever disaster occurred.

I remember that he lives in downtown Los Angeles, but I didn't realize that he lived in one of those old department stores that are now apartments and condos. There's an interesting blue tile on the outside, something that I'm sure he knows the history of.

"Do you want to come upstairs?" Max asks me, nodding at the building. I'm torn between staring at his ass and wanting to throw myself down the staircase.

"Yeah, sure," I say, agreeing just to extend the evening.

"Fun fact," he says, climbing up the stairs.

This entire night was a disaster, and this dating plan was so stupid. I'm barely listening as Max continues the third fun fact he's given me since we drove home. First was a strange story about how the first traffic alert system in Los Angeles was developed for nuclear war, and the second was something about how a movie starring Hayden Christensen made him want to be a journalist. This one, it seems, is about his apartment. "This used to be one of the largest department stores on the West Coast. The change in parking requirements and some seismic retrofitting are why downtown is cool again."

"Don't tell my mom. She's still terrified, and she moved here in the 1980s," I say. "Earthquakes are terrifying." It's a sentence that usually ends a conversation or contributes enough that I don't have to worry about adding more, but Max sees it as an opening for more questions.

"What's the first earthquake you remember?" He opens his door, and his apartment is...quaint. I take in a collection of coffee cups with the local PBS station's logo, a set of slippers, and what looks to be a scroll on the doorframe right as I walk in.

"Uh, I dunno. Northridge." I'm still taking in the location, struck by the lack of multicolored lights that have always been a constant in my friends' apartments and my own in December.

"Oh, that was in 1994, so that means you're—" before he can take a guess at my age, I tap him on the shoulder to interrupt. He whirls around, adjusts his glasses, and quirks an eyebrow at me.

"We shouldn't do this," I say, voicing the thought that's been rattling around in my brain since we left bingo night. "It's an idea that only works in movies and young adult novels. I have no right to bring you into this." I'm chewing my lip so I don't say more, don't let him know that I'm bad at being a girlfriend in my actual life, let alone in my *Harriet the Spy* alter ego life.

"No," Max replies confidently.

"No?"

"No." He crosses the living room, kicking off his shoes near the end table where they join a pile of other shoes that look similarly well worn. "No. You never give up on a story the first time. Do you really think we would have found out about Watergate if Deep Throat had decided to not show up the first time?"

Deep Throat. I googled that for a college class on media studies and discovered an entirely different bit of history. "Uh, no?"

"So we won't stop for this. We just need a different approach to the situation."

"So not fake dating?" I'm relieved that I won't have to keep up this farce, but there's a jolt of disappointment that bounces through me and settles low in my stomach, like I've eaten a bad dish of seafood.

"No, no." Max has taken up residence on his couch. There's a pile of dog-eared books next to it and a ring where a glass goes. His side, his space. Not for the first time, I notice there's a method to Max's chaos. "The fake dating is a good idea—sit *down*, Brooklyn, you're giving me hives; relax, *please*—but I think we need to refine our story."

"Refine our story?" I sit on the edge of the couch, one butt cheek off, awkwardly perching. There's nothing relaxing about this situation. There's nothing relaxing about this entire fucking evening. Nothing has felt relaxed since the moment I started working at ConservTech.

"Yes." Max reaches across to the *other* stack of books on the coffee table. He grabs one and flips through, muttering to himself. *Wrong,* he mumbles. He tosses the book to another pile and finds another one. When he reaches, the hem of his sweater pulls up, exposing a slice of skin at his lower back along with just a hint of the elastic band of his briefs. My eyes snap to it, and I find myself curious as to what type of underwear he wears.

My inappropriate and unnecessary train of thought is interrupted when Max finds what he's been looking for.

In America, the president reigns for four years, and journalism governs forever and ever. – Oscar Wilde

"We just have to do better at being a couple," Max says, like being a couple is as easy as blowing a bubble or skipping. Something every six-year-old in California can do.

"What does that look like?"

"Well, we should know basic things about each other," Max says, beginning a list with a pencil and notepad that he pulls out of the couch like it belongs to Mary Poppins. "Birthdate, place of birth, college, allergies."

"You'll need to know star signs, too." Max gives me a weird look. "What? It's Los Angeles. Should probably do our entire birth chart, rising signs and moon signs, all of that."

"Fine," Max says, and I decide that I like to make him flustered. Just to mess with him, I'm going to become an expert on Zodiac. He continues his list. "If you had chicken pox as a kid, who you voted for in the last few local elections—"

"How you kiss," I add. Max looks up from his list and makes eye contact with me.

I let out a nervous giggle. "Just kidding," I say, giving a smile even I know is weird. It's too toothy and my lips feel weird, or maybe it's because my mouth has gone a bit dry.

"No, no." He has put down the notepad but tucked the pencil behind his ear. It's easy to imagine him as being from a hundred years ago, barking down the hallway with typewriters clattering around him. "That's a great idea." A chill runs through my entire body when his eyes flick down to my lips and he takes his glasses off. I think he's going to lean toward me, but he simply pinches the bridge of his nose.

"Well, what are you like?" I'm not much of a drinker, but I kind of wish I had a glass of wine. Maybe it would break this awkwardness and let the words flow a bit more easily.

"I'd like to think I'm, well, *attentive* to my partner's needs," Max says, and he places his glasses back on his nose.

"Partner?" I question.

"The person I am, well, um, *engaged* with." This is wonderful. Max is usually confident, pulling a quote or a tip or a fact out every second. There are times this evening I wondered when he had time to breathe in order to continue, but he's tongue-tied now. He's turning a light pink, and he keeps licking his lips like it's Santa Ana season.

He's nervous.

I *love* it.

"You?" He looks over at me, and then I don't feel so smug anymore. Because I'm nervous now that I'm under his journalistic microscope.

"Same," I say, and even as the word is leaving my mouth, I know he's not going to let a one-word answer go.

"Same as what?"

"I like making my partner feel good."

"What makes you feel good?" He's quick with a follow-up question.

"Um." Now it's my turn to be speechless.

He reaches for his glasses again. I imagine that, this time, the nose pinch is going to be accompanied by a frustrated sigh.

"You know, the usual. A little bit of this, a little bit of that."

"Hmm," Max says and folds his glasses. He places them to the side on top of the open book he just read from. "You know, there's a journalistic standard for this."

I shoot him a side-eye. "There's an entry in *Strunk and White* about kissing?"

He chuckles, and I feel a flare of pride in my chest for pulling a laugh out of such a serious man.

"No, Brooklyn. Of course not. Though Strunk did have three children, so." He pumps his eyebrows once, and I laugh. "No, it's an extension of what we're doing already."

I know what he's getting at, so I continue to defer. "Making a list?"

And *there's* the exasperated sigh. He's fun to poke at. "It's part of our cover. We have to get better at kissing."

"I am *perfectly* adequate at kissing. More than fine. I get top marks. A-plus. Five stars." At least I hope so.

Max rolls his eyes. "We have to get better at kissing *each other*."

Oh.

And as I take in Max's body, one ankle kicked over on his thigh, arms behind his head, a smug smirk on his face, the one curl that insists on going a different direction than the rest, I'm grateful for his commitment to journalism.

Because the fact of the matter—

The headline—

The lede—

Is that I want to kiss Max right now.

I want to kiss Max *a lot*.

Max is continuing to talk about the importance of a convincing cover story in undercover journalism and that we need to define how we met and how we know each other, but I can't stop thinking about kissing him.

"Max." I put a hand on his arm, and he stops talking for a second. "Can I kiss you?" I swallow over the lump in my throat.

His eyes flick down to my lips. In a move I know works on a couch as well as at a bar, I run my tongue slowly across my lower lips and track how his eyes follow the movement.

"Yes."

"For journalism," I add.

He snorts. "Now that's a line." Then there's a moment, a bit of tension, a string pulled taut. I reach across the expanse of the couch and place my hand on his cheek. My lips follow, and I press a light kiss to the corner of his lips. He turns his head, and our lips meet.

It's a bit awkward in the beginning, the way all kisses are. Our lips aren't even quite aligned at first, and there are a few moments where neither of us is sure who is supposed to move their lips first. I nip, just a bit, and Max's lips respond in turn. The kiss stays simple, sweet even, and I content myself with the thought that this will be the kind of kiss that can convince my coworkers that we're dating.

And then Max's hands frame my jaw, the tips of his fingers brushing against my hairline. He opens his mouth a smidge wider, and the tip of his tongue traces against my upper lip. It unlocks something in me, because, while he's not the type of guy I would approach in a bar or eye on the street, this uptight, serious, frustrating man *gets* to me.

Maybe it's that he takes me seriously.

Maybe it's that he secretly shares some of my cockeyed optimism.

Shit, maybe it's that he looks a bit like Seth Cohen from *The O.C.*

Whatever it is, the first brush of our tongues against each other confirms that I've developed a crush on Max.

My hand is still on his cheek, and I slide it into his hair, curling my fingers and tugging just a bit. I'm rewarded when Max moans into my mouth. Then he leaves my lips and presses kisses down my neck, licking at my pulse.

"Over here," he gently commands, pulling at the waistband of my slacks until I've straddled him. I brace my hands on the back of the couch and take a moment to study Max. His lips are red, his hair has grown about two inches. It's not the only thing that's growing, if what

I'm feeling between my legs is any indication. We're both breathing hard, that type of frantic *are we doing this?* that accompanies a really fucking great kiss. And as if to answer the unspoken question floating in the air between us, he cups my jaw and pulls me forward.

His hand is crawling up my back toward my bra clasp, and my hips are moving in tiny motions—forward, back, side to side—and I feel pleasure beginning to build in that tight space between my hip bones, in my lower back. Max is sucking on my lower lip. Just when I think he's going to twist his fingers and unsnap the clasp, he goes totally still underneath me. Taking my cue from him, I stop moving. I pull my hands out of his hair and slide off his lap.

"We can't do this," he says, in an echo of my words from earlier.

"Oh, okay." I can't keep up with the way this man vacillates. The way he moves from confident journalist to shy flirt to the person who steals the breath from my mouth with his own. To someone who is backing out.

"Not the dating thing. Not the story," he clarifies. "I can't sleep with a source." I have an impulse to correct him, but I know I'm wrong. For a moment, I wasn't a source and he wasn't the person helping me do the right thing. We were just two bodies chasing pleasure. I want to argue and tell him that maybe I wasn't going to sleep with him, but I know—*we* know—exactly where this evening would have headed if he hadn't slammed on the brakes.

"Right." I adjust my hair. I twist it up into a messy bun and then immediately pull my hair tie out and let my hair down again.

"Um." He rummages around in the couch and finds his notepad under his hip. The top page is crinkled. I knocked his pencil out from behind his ear when I ran my hands through his hair the first time, so I lean over and pick it up from the floor.

"Here."

"Thanks. Um," he repeats. "We should still continue with PDA, of course."

"For the story."

"For the story."

"But we can't act on this." He waves a hand between us.

"Right," I say with a sigh. I know in my heart that he's right. I trust his experience in doing the correct thing, but I'd be lying if I said I wasn't disappointed.

"Brooklyn," he says. My name sounds different from before. It's not the exasperated or questioning *Brooklyn* of our diner chats, but gentle. Soft. Affectionate. "This story matters. It's bigger than us."

"Of course." I take the pencil and notepad from him and scribble a few ideas down. We spend another few minutes being incredibly stilted around each other before I decide to default to complaining about traffic and get up to leave.

"I'm a Libra sun, Scorpio moon, and a Cap rising," I say, sliding my shoes back on by the door. I can feel his unique brand of playful annoyance rising, and that feels like something right, putting us firmly back into the category of...whatever we were before The Kiss. He walks me down to the lobby, and I step out into the cool evening air. Out here, the light scent of salt water mingles with the exhaust from the ever-present traffic. Los Angeles at its finest.

"Good night, Brooklyn. Let me know when you get home."

"Of course, Max." I give him a salute with two fingers. I'm almost to the corner of the sidewalk when he clears his throat from the doorway. The halogen hallway light is shining on him, tossing bits of light off his curls, which are even more mussed from my hands.

"I'm an Aquarius," he says. "I'll find out my other signs." We share a soft chuckle, and he heads back into his building.

Harriet the Spy did not prepare me for what to do when I develop a crush on my coconspirator.

Chapter 12

One of the best things about Max is that the day after I leave his house, hot and bothered and feeling equal parts guilty and turned on, he's all business. I get a text from him at eight in the morning, as I'm looking at my coffeepot.

Max: Are we still on for tonight?

I peek at the whiteboard calendar that Gemma and I keep updated with everything that's going on. For the vast majority of the past few years, it's been a record of all of Gemma's events and the occasional date that I had that went nowhere. I did add all the corporate events to it last week in a fit of organization.

White elephant reads today's square.

Brooklyn: Yes.

What I want to say is "Yes, and also, are we cool? Because I almost used your lap to get myself off before I realized that I was letting what I wanted get in the way of the overwhelmingly huge desire to feel like I'm a part of something." And that would not be cool and chill and that is what I am attempting to be. Cool and chill Brooklyn.

Max: Excellent. Where is it?

It turns out that the event is at a brewpub down the street, one of a million places in LA that have embraced industrial chic, which means expensive, overly hazy beers and metal stools that remind me of a mid-century hospital. Fun. My thumb hovers over my phone screen. I want to cancel, to drown my tears in a cup of tea and rewatch an entire season of *Survivor*, but it's Max. And he's excited about everything in regard to this project, so I sigh and text back the address.

Max: Noted. I've been researching white elephant.

Brooklyn: Max, it's not a big deal. You don't even have to show up.

Max: Nope. Something about tonight feels good.

Anything is better than the way I felt last night, so I agree.

Work is the same, though Max takes to texting me once an hour with guesses as to what I've brought as a white elephant gift. He's much more creative than I am, seeing as that I just found a terrible mug at a tourist gift store and filled it with seven small bottles of 99 Bananas.

Carlina, Vee, and I have hit that three o'clock slump that has accompanied me to every job I've ever had, that moment where you've done all your necessary tasks for the day, eaten lunch, and gotten tired, and you don't have the energy to be ambitious and start on tomorrow's tasks.

"Are you going tonight?" I ask.

"Well, considering that I like my job and don't want our department to be cut, yeah," Carlina responds.

"What did you bring as a gift?" Vee asks me.

"I'm not telling," I respond, shocked. "I bet you're the type of person that tries to get someone to tell you if you have them for Secret Santa!"

"Speaking of," Carlina says, rolling her chair over to me. "Vee and I always opt out of the company Secret Snowflake because I don't actually like that many people here and there's no way they'd know what to give me." She shudders. "One year, I got a donation to the LAPD in my name, so..."

"We do something with our department and our partners that we've termed Secret Satan," Vee grins at me. "Are you and Max in? The goal is to get the person you've pulled the most hideous T-shirt possible, which we have to wear at the bar we go to."

"Uh, I'll ask Max tonight," I say, my cheeks blushing. It's the first time that I'll have seen him since we made out, and I'm nervous. Texting is one thing, but being in the same space is something else.

The workday is monotonous, unless you count the inspired lunchtime debate about the relative merits of Andi's boyfriend in *The Devil Wears Prada* (Vee and I were firmly on the side that he was a piece of shit, while Carlina, inexplicably, thought that his ability to make a grilled cheese was worth all the toxicity). We've just maneuvered to the conference room—the same one we had to navigate during the bingo game—when my phone buzzes.

Max: Hello, girlfriend.

Max: I have arrived with my secret gift.

I walk over to the elevator to head down to the lobby to meet him, but I feel a presence as I approach the buttons. Aron has rounded the corner, a glass of brown liquid in his hand, and his hair is a bit disheveled.

"Hi, Aron," I say, tapping the button and praying to all the gods of Christmas that he's not heading to the elevator. "Going down?"

"Not that I don't want to," he says, lechery seeping out of his pores for just a second, "but I'm headed to the office."

"No party?" I fake pout and hate myself for it.

"Busy tonight," he says, and that same tickle in the back of my brain occurs again.

"Big deal you're trying to close?" I really lean into the femininity in my voice, make him think I'm stupider than I am. Gemma and my women's studies professors would have my ass if they knew what I was doing.

"Not that. It's just that, well, business is a competition, right?" He laughs, even though the mission of the company is that *a rising tide lifts all boats*. "I hire a firm that tracks searches into our financial records and business dealings, and they've noticed an uptick in suspicious activity over the past two weeks."

Resisting the urge to pump my fist in victory, I make a confused face. "Why would anyone do this? Hostile foreign actors?"

"Most likely an upstart company. We'll absorb them in a few months, then fire their staff." He laughs. His cockiness is as infuriating as it is infatuating, and I am quite literally saved by the bell when the elevator rings.

"I'd love to hear more sometime," I flirt back over my shoulder, but I'm not sure if he heard me, as he's looking at his phone again. Once in the elevator, I tap out a few notes in my phone so I remember them.

Max is in the lobby with an oblong object wrapped in two reusable grocery bags. Deciding that I don't think things can be more awkward than they already are, I ask him if he brought a dildo to the white elephant.

"No, Brooklyn," he says, giving me that teacher glare I've started to realize I love to worm out of him. "All my research says that the best white elephant gift is something lying around your house. Do you really think I have a three-foot-long dildo lying around? And if so, why would I regift it?" He shudders. "Gross." I spend the entire ride up trying to guess what's in the package before he decides to lecture me about how the name "white elephant" comes from a legend about a gift to a Thai king.

"Hey, Max," Vee says as we leave the elevator. I duck quickly away to grab my present, hastily wrapped in a leftover Amazon Prime box, and come back to see Max laughing with Carlina and a few other people I've managed to get regular lunches or after-work hangs with.

I feel a touch of awkwardness as I watch them. If everything goes according to plan, what happens to all of them? Will I lose this tentative new group of friends? Will I lose Max?

As a friend, of course.

Brenda, with her saccharine sweet grin and sparkly Santa hat, organizes everyone into a series of small groups to compete. Max pouts next to me.

"Now you love Christmas?" I whisper to him.

"No, this way it's less likely there'll be a good gift in my circle. I'm Jewish. Come on, I love a good deal," Max chuckles back, then shifts over to the circle he's been assigned to.

I'm struck again by the fact that I don't know *how* to react. One time, my sister brought home a boyfriend to meet our mom. He spent the entire evening ranting about how immigrants were ruining this country, not knowing that our stepdad was Mexican, though light skinned. Eventually, my mom took his half-finished plate from him and kindly asked him to leave our house, all Great Lakes passive aggressiveness. Then she told Hazel that if she ever dated anyone like that again, she could kiss all the family benefits goodbye. The entire dinner, I just sat there, sweating, knowing that I should say something, that I could do it, but I didn't. I'm the person they make *see something, say something*, reminders for, because I see something, worry, and never do anything about it.

I give myself a mental reminder that I need to do some googling tonight. *How to support your Jewish fake boyfriend while you attempt*

CORPORATE MANDATED HOLIDAY ROMANCE 87

to break a news story. I'll find a podcast or a well-designed Instagram page like a good millennial.

I'm barely paying attention to my own circle, other than to open a flat rectangular package that ends up being a *Supernatural* calendar. Ha. Joke's on whoever put that in. I love *Supernatural*. I love the gift a bit less when I realize the calendar is from 2006, but I can always cross out the dates. I'm trying to chat to the person next to me, who I know works in the business office, thinking that it could be a good contact, but they're about as interesting as a manila folder. Practical but ultimately useless.

"We did just update to a new operating system for our benefits," he says when he's interrupted by a group of people laughing from Max's circle.

"A toilet plunger?" A woman who I recognize from data analysis is saying. "This is the best gift. It's practical as hell!"

"It's the correct kind, too," Max is saying. I start laughing when I realize that it was *his* gift. "Fun fact: most people have a sink plunger instead of a proper one for the toilet."

"He's funny," the guy next to me is saying. "Does he work here?"

"No, he's, uh." I wait for a second. "He's my boyfriend, actually."

"Hmm," he says, noncommittal. "Lucky."

I think I am.

After the game has ended and the bar is opened, I find my way over to Max. I've been hyping myself up over the past ten minutes to ask him if we're fine, but something different comes out of my mouth. "So how did you get into journalism?" I ask when Carlina has headed off to try to bribe Steven to give her the mug that says *office bitch*.

"I'd like to tell you it's because of my religion's deep quest for knowledge and search for truth, that I was descended from rabbinical scholars," he laughs into his tea. "But I just like storytelling, and I've never found fiction to be worth my time when there are stories out there that are *real*." I can hear the awe in his voice. I imagine the way that a younger Max would have been making homemade newspapers to pass out in his neighborhood.

"That's cool," I say, at a loss for what to add.

"I think so," he says, nudging me with his shoulder. "Plus, I get to meet the coolest people. I recently met this woman named Brooklyn Peters, who is trying to save the world."

I roll my eyes and say no to Vee, who's begging me to go out for karaoke.

"I need my beauty sleep!" I call back.

"Max?" Vee asks.

"She needs her beauty sleep," he echoes, looping his arm through mine.

"Doubt you'll get that much sleep," Carlina stage whispers as we pick up our gifts. We walk out to the parking lot together, my new/old calendar under my arm and Max's set of four plastic Jimmy Buffett memorial margarita glasses under his. We're next to my car, and I can see Max's down the row.

"Thanks for coming tonight," I say. "I hope it was helpful."

"I connected with some people who I think will have a lot to say," he responds. "Brooklyn, I just wanted to say—"

But I interrupt him when I remember. "Oh! Right before I got you from the lobby, I ran into Aron."

"And?" Max raises an eyebrow.

"He told me that the company has been recently searched a lot? Apparently there are other companies he hires to track that?" I pull out my phone and show him the notes I tapped out. He takes a photo of the screen on his own.

"I have some connections at those companies," he says thoughtfully. "There are some delightful sleeper agents in some of those big, evil places."

"Like me," I joke.

"Like you," he replies seriously. And he's so kind and genuine that I finally ask it.

"Are we good? After, well—" My voice trails off as I lose the small burst of courage.

"Brooklyn, we've always been good," he replies. "I don't lie to you." He grazes my arm and squeezes my hand once, and then he heads to his car.

Chapter 13

"Do you know all the best Christmas songs were written by Jews?" is the greeting Max gives me as I show up at his apartment in order to run a short cram session on Christmas movies and songs.

"Hello to you, too," I respond, getting used to the way Max greets me with a fact.

"I was doing some research," he says, grinning and looking all too proud of himself. When Aron is smug, it makes me want to grit my teeth and figure out a way to set fire to our building. When Max is smug, it makes me want to give him a kiss on the cheek and a smack on the ass, neither of which is appropriate for the subtle friendship that we've settled into.

"Okay, it's wonderful that you know the classics, but do you know the best-selling Christmas song?"

"White Christmas?"

I make a buzzer sound to let him know he's wrong. "It's Mariah Carey's 'All I Want for Christmas is You,' and if you say one negative thing about that song, then I will leave right now."

Max holds up his hands in mock surrender and laughs. "You're fine, you're fine."

I walk in holding a plastic bin that was left over from one of Gemma's frequent organizing bins and a box of Cranberry ginger ale that never fails to make me think of Christmas dinners when I was young. I set the beer on the counter and shake the box like I'm trying to figure out what present is inside.

"What is that?" Max asks, skeptically.

"Today is song training, right?" He nods, confirming. "I thought that instead of just working through a playlist, we could play a game? You pick a song title and try to guess what it's about, and then we listen to it and see if you're right?" When I say it out loud, it sounds *so* stupid. But Max grins, a full, face-splitting smile that's new.

"Like a riddle!"

"Of course you'd like riddles," I say to suppress my glee.

"Do you need ice?" he asks.

"That'd be lovely."

Taking out a speaker from my bag, I play some music from my Christmas playlist. In the background, track seven of the *Charlie Brown Christmas* album plays while Max shuffles around his kitchen and comes back with two tumblers.

"What's this one called?" he asks, handing me a glass.

"Skating," I say. "It never fails to make me tear up." Max cocks his head. It's a movement I've learned means *tell me more*. "There's something about it that captures how it feels to be a little kid at Christmas. Like, even though I've never experienced a first snow or gone sledding, I can imagine being outside and feeling as if the world is my playground. No worries about rent or the cost of eggs or, I don't know, being an investigative journalist—"

"Hey, I played journalist as a kid!" he interjects.

I chuckle. "Of course you did. I dunno, and I'm sure it's a part of, like, Christian white privilege, but Christmastime felt freeing in a way that not even summer vacation did. There's food and family and toys and movies and so much candy." A beat. "It was so exciting."

"It's like the last *Calvin & Hobbes* comic," Max says, then pulls up the image on his phone. I take a moment to study it. *Let's go exploring.* The cartoon excitement matches how I felt when Max offered this opportunity.

"Exactly," I reply and we have a moment where we share a soft smile while jazz plays in the background. All that's needed is a roaring fireplace, so I turn on Max's TV and put on a four-hour video of a yule log.

"Setting the mood," he laughs, pouring his ginger ale.

"Okay, pick," I say, putting the box on Max's lap. He gingerly picks a slip out and reads it.

"This is an easy one. Even I know 'White Christmas.'" He thinks for a moment. "It's good. Schmaltzy. Would be like a jug of wine."

I chuckle. "Fine, pick again."

He makes a huge production of finding another slip of paper. Pulls it out and reads it, his eyebrows pulling together in his thinking face. I've come to terms with the fact that I have a crush on Max. So I realize that sometimes (okay, most of the time), I look at him in a way that I would never look at a friend. Like I am now. His lips are pursed, and I want to kiss them, but it's the way his eyebrows and forehead communicate his thought processes that I like the most. A scrunch, a stretch, a raise. The most frustrating part of this crush is that I don't even just think he's attractive—though I've known it from the first time I saw him. What's frustrating is how much I like his brain and the way it approaches the world.

"I don't know this one," Max says slowly.

"Title?" I swipe on my phone to the playlist I've prepared.

"'Do They Know It's Christmas,'" he says slowly. I cringe internally and think about how Max is going to *hate* this song. And I'm correct, because after the first chorus, we can't even hear the words because Max is talking about the legacy of religious colonialism. All things I agree with, but the way he's building on his own rants makes me chuckle into my ginger ale.

"Okay, so we won't add that to the dating playlist." Max laughs.

"Oh, this is about a church," Max guesses. I play the song, laughing. "Not exactly."

"It's about *shopping*?"

"Capitalism is a major part of Christmas, I guess."

"Oh, this is easy. This small child, who is clearly delusional, wants the most dangerous animal in Africa to be placed under a tree."

"A nice gift of shoes for your child."

I have tears rolling down my face as Max takes in the lyrics. "What the *hell*? This is about a kid's mom *dying*?"

"Played on the radio all the time when I was younger. Wild, uh?"

"Mom's having an affair? Isn't that a sin, Brook?" Then, later, "*Oh*, it's the kid's dad. Okay, that one is kind of cute."

"Did Santa have a kid?" Then, after the music starts. "Oh, this is a sexy song." His eyebrows flick up. "Is this for, like, a Christmas striptease? It has very similar vibes to when Marilyn Monroe sang to Kennedy."

"'Last Christmas'? Uh, that's easy. It's about last year. At Christmas."

"You're right," I say. "But this is one of the best songs ever." I play the Wham! Version, and Max is bobbing his head and nodding, but then halfway through, I switch to the version done by Jimmy Eat World that I first discovered when a boy in high school burned it onto a CD for me. "This is an even better version." I take a moment and worry that I'm going to get maudlin and dramatic, but *fuck it*. "I think the best types of Christmas songs aren't really about the holiday or religion—though 'O Holy Night' can really hit when sung well—they're about community and family and feeling comfortable." I take a sip of my ginger ale. "A good Christmas song works across the generations and across the styles."

Max looks at me thoughtfully. "I like that."

I like you. "Thanks."

"When we finally sell this story, our next one can be on how a good Christmas song transcends space and time." I'm flattered by the way that, even if he's joking, he sees some kind of future with us. Having wormed our way into each other's lives for this amount of time makes me want to stay in Max's sphere and keep him in mine.

"I think we're good on songs," I say suddenly to shift the subject. "Holiday movies?"

"Can we skip movies?" Max whines, sprawling out on the couch.

"Only if we can order pizza," I respond.

"I will bribe you with carbs and cheese if it means I don't have to suffer through the meaning of Christmas." Max swipes on his phone and orders pizza from an app. "Oh, and by the way, I did some digging. I think we might have a break in the story."

I spring up from where I've been lounging on the armrest. "Excuse me? What? And you let me subject you to this nonsense game of guess what the song is about? Who gives a fuck about Christmas shoes when you've got updates?"

He chuckles. "Nothing is going to change in a day, Brook. I figured we'd get to it." He details how he's been researching the shell companies ConservTech uses in different jurisdictions and states and who their contracts are accountable to. After about three minutes, my eyes start to glaze over. "Brooklyn?"

"I'm listening!" I lie.

"Chatting with Micah was really helpful. She was willing to go on the record about some files she had to shift and some weird accounts she's noticed over the past few years."

"Fuck yes," I say, though I'm internally disappointed that I'm not the one who provided the critical information to Max.

Larger goal. It's not about me.

"Thanks for inviting me to that white elephant," he says.

"Hey, maybe I just knew that I really needed a new plunger."

"As annoying as your company is, your friends are really fun."

Friends.

Chapter 14

It's become routine over the past few days, Max stopping by my office. At first, it was just to drop off a coffee or a lunch, both things I insisted on paying him back for. He started to linger more, and we started to plan. Instead of him waiting for me at the front desk, he'd say he would just drop something off to me. A chance to get lost, to understand the layout of the offices. I started paying attention, too. I realized that Aron took a break every morning around ten, a fact I texted to Max in a separate app, one with disappearing messages that makes me really feel like a spy. The next time he came around, it was easy for him to take a wrong turn and "accidentally" end up in the office space beside Aron's. I did some poking around on the internal website and realized that was the CFO's office, another fact I squirreled away in my brain for later.

So it was easy—perhaps too easy—for Max to get roped into our weekly marketing department outing. It wasn't one of the staid and stoic "corporate mandated fun times," but rather something we had started doing over the past few weeks. One of us would get an especially frustrating email from another department asking the design team to "just make it pop," and within seconds, a group text would go out with the name of a bar or an activity. The best and worst part about living in Los Angeles is that there is no shortage of things to do. And for someone who suffers from terminal FOMO, I'm always willing to go along with a group plan. In the last week alone, I've been mini golfing in what used to be an airplane hangar and I've been to a *Lord of the Rings* Brewery.

"All right, time to pull out the big guns," Carlina says, clicking her mouse so aggressively that even Vee looks up from under their noise-canceling headphones.

"Oh," they say, knowingly whipping out their phone to type out a text message.

"Invite the old crew," Carlina says. "We need people who understand this shit." She gives me a pointed look, like I wouldn't understand the complexities of the office. I've been playing my cards close to my chest, but I still meet with Aron once a week, and I know that pisses her off.

"Listen, I don't know how to balance all of this—" I begin, but Vee cuts me off.

"Invite your boyfriend," they say. "I'm bringing my partner. Carlina usually invites her boyfriend too when we need to really let off steam this way."

"Oh, okay," I respond, feeling that warmth in my stomach that tends to foreshadow a new friend. I type out a quick text to Max informing him that we're headed out to a bar called L'Etage and that we'll be there at seven. He replies with a series of emojis that involve a winking face, an exploding heart, and a microphone. He's still impossible.

Turns out, his emojis were more on the nose than I expected, because L'Etage is a karaoke bar.

Once again showing his uncanny ability to transport himself throughout the maze of Los Angeles highways, Max is waiting outside the bar when I get there. He's got a book in one hand and his head tipped down. He's cast perfectly in the glow of a streetlight like something out of a historic photo.

"Hey," I say, ducking my head slightly to see what he's reading. I don't get a good look at the title, but it seems like something that's beyond what I would usually read. I highly doubt that Max is reading true crime or thrillers in his spare time.

"Hello, girlfriend," he says, giving me a half smile. I resist the urge to roll my eyes, annoyed at the way I enjoy being claimed by him, even if it's a bit fake. "This is an interesting choice for the evening."

"What would you have done instead, stayed at home and done the crossword?"

"I'll have you know, I'm excellent at the crossword," he says.

I continue to push and prod, tease and tickle. "I bet you do your crossword in pen, huh? Anything else would be cheating?"

The slight blush that spreads across Max's cheeks lets me know that I've guessed correctly. I could continue to make fun of him, but honestly, I'm proud of his confidence. I don't like using pen for anything, because plans change, or I change my mind, and that scribble over words or appointments or even a missed guess on a crossword clue reminds me that I've failed.

Max probably doesn't fail.

"Let's go inside," he says, putting his book in his messenger bag and placing a hand on my lower back to guide me through the door. We head up to the bar, and I scan the room, looking for my coworkers.

"Should we ask some questions tonight?" I ask, having failed to get the bartender's attention. Max pulls his lip between his teeth and

CORPORATE MANDATED HOLIDAY ROMANCE   99

considers for a second. I fill the silence between us. "I mean, if people get a bit drunk, then they might be willing to talk more?"

"It's unethical to interview someone when they're drunk," Max says. "There are some issues around consent and recording."

I wave to the bartender again, still failing to get her attention. "Well, yeah, that makes sense, but also, isn't it unethical to lie about our relationship?" Max gets his Thoughtful Look on his face, the one where his vision goes a bit hazy and he looks off into the distance, as if the answer to the inane question is somewhere a few yards in front of us.

"I mean, at this point, I don't know if it's even—" Whatever Max is going to say is cut off when the bartender appears in front of us. Max orders a local craft beer for himself and a cider for me, the drinks we ordered last time. He remembers. He starts a tab and hands the cider over to me.

"What were you saying?" I ask, shouting a bit as the volume turns up a bit. The karaoke host is readying their speakers, testing a mic.

"Nothing," he replies. He opens his mouth to add on to that, but snaps it shut. Takes a sip of beer and swallows. "There are your friends," he says.

I want to correct him, tell him *they're just coworkers*, but I can't ignore the way I get excited when Vee and Carlina wave to me from the table they've commandeered. Max and I make our way through the crowd. Immediately, I turn down Carlina's offer of a shot, but I scan the QR code on the table to pull up the song options. I try not to smile too much as I look through the listings and find that they have my favorite karaoke song. It's long and it's obnoxious. And, if I know my coworkers—*friends*—they'll love it as much as I do. I look over at Max, who is scrolling through his phone too quickly to be looking at the karaoke songs. I assume he's scrolling whatever app he uses to keep himself updated on the news, toggling between the BBC and NPR to some other major news site to see how different areas of the world cover the same news story.

"Who's up first?" Vee says, sipping on their margarita.

I want to volunteer. I want to be the girl who gets on stage first, but I'm always the one who waits. I never went first or second during presentations at school, preferring to let someone else set the tone. I'm never the first one to jump in the ocean. No, I wait for a friend to go first. That way they'll take the brunt of any stingrays that may be under the sand.

"Brooklyn would love to," Max says for me. Again, that impulse to argue is replaced by the knowledge that Max is right.

"Yeah, Manhattan?" Carlina says, taking back a shot like it's water.

"She loves going first," he says, settling a hand on my thigh under the table. Instantly, I have no desire to move anywhere, not with his hand on me like this.

"Sure," I say, rolling my eyes. I log on to the karaoke website using my phone and tap in the series of numbers that will get this song going. I haven't sung in public since before lockdown. I sang in my high school choir and participated in a few musicals, but now I mostly keep my singing to the rush of traffic on Sepulveda.

Idle small talk and chatter settles over the group as another singer gets called up. A bearded man in a flannel who does an enthusiastic version of "Goodbye Earl."

"All right, next up, we've got Brooklyn!" the host shouts.

"What are you singing?" Max asks. I grin back at him in response. It's fun to keep him guessing.

The opening bars of Paramore's "Crushcrushcrush" ring out over the speakers, and I wonder if I've played my hand too early. Is this song a little too on the nose for how I feel about Max? It's fun to be the girl who gets on stage first, even if my voice cracks a bit on the opening lyric and I squawk out a note at the end. Until now, I'd forgotten the way that being the center of attention gives me just enough of a dopamine hit to make my blood buzz and my breathing speed up.

It's not unlike how I feel after an orgasm.

I shove that thought down as I hand the microphone back to the host and wave to the crowd. I make my way over to the table and flop down next to Max, snatching his glass of water as I do so. Like an actual girlfriend would do.

"You're really good," he says, his lips parted as he regards me.

"Nah," I say, deflecting the compliment.

"Fuck you," Carlina yells across the table. "That was actually good."

"Thanks." I can feel my cheeks begin to heat, and Max makes a disgruntled noise next to me. He nudges my arm and waves his phone at me.

Max: It's too loud in here for me to talk.

But I like it when you have to get close to me to speak.

Brooklyn: We could leave?

Max: You're having fun.

Brooklyn: I have a soft spot for a good karaoke bar. I think song choices say a lot about a person.

Max: You looked really sexy up there singing.

I'm grateful for how loud it is now. A woman with curly black hair is screaming an emo anthem I vaguely remember from a mix CD a high school boyfriend made for me. I'm also grateful it's dim inside the bar so Max can't see how my eyes are wide and my face is flushed.

You're just saying it to keep up with the facade, I type back.

Max gives me a disappointed look. He begins typing a sentence—*I don't...*—then deletes it. An ironic victory, that I'm right. He's just saying things to be nice to me. He doesn't actually compliment me—

Suddenly, his hand is on my thigh again, the heat of his palm permeating the fabric of my jeans. Then he's moving the hair that was over my ear to the side. "Brooklyn," he says, his breath hot against my neck in a way that causes goose bumps to spring up all over my body. "I don't lie to you."

After another round for the table—which has grown; a former intern for the marketing department that has changed companies but apparently is still friends with Vee has appeared—I've definitely surpassed my usual limit. I turn to ask Max how he's getting home to find he's not there.

The opening bass line of Beastie Boys' "Sabotage" start to play. It's obvious the entire bar is feeling good, because everyone joins in. It's that kind of scream-singing to the music that can only be accomplished in the shower or in a group setting. I let out a *whoo* that tells me I'm going to need an extra-large breakfast burrito tomorrow morning and turn around to see who is on stage.

It's Max.

Max, who has another full beer in his left hand, grabs the microphone with his right and wraps the cord around his fist like he's a professional. His hair is messy, like he's been running his hand through it, and the ends curl more than I'm used to. The top three buttons of his shirt are undone, and while I expect to see a crisp white undershirt, I realize that I can see his collarbones and a hint of his chest.

I want to tell him to button up his shirt so no one else sees, then pull him into a back room and tear the buttons off myself.

I want to lick my way up his throat.

He scans the crowd as he takes a breath. Just before he starts the song, his eyes land on me. He grins, a wicked one that promises a variety of things he could do with that mouth.

And then he begins to sing. If you can call screaming along with Ad-Rock singing.

He moves more than I've ever seen, twisting and dancing around the stage in that way so many white boys do, all odd angles and arms akimbo. He's surprisingly magnetic, and the bar has taken notice.

"Your boyfriend is full of surprises," Vee says. They stick their fingers into their mouth and let out a loud whistle.

"He certainly is."

"He's fucking hot, too," Carlina's boyfriend—Jordan?—says. "Do you ever share?" Carlina gives him a playful slap on the wrist, but the heat in both of their eyes tells me that wasn't just a joke.

I've had friends who were poly or swung or were ethically non-monogamous—it's LA, you meet all sorts of people—but when it comes to Max, I find I'm feeling selfish. Like these people should be lucky I even share him with them in a platonic respect.

When the song ends, Max plops down next to me, his hair curling even more now that he's worked up from singing. "This is fun! I haven't been out like this in a long time."

"Me neither," I say, breathless in a way that makes it feel like I just got off the stage, too. He leans in, just an inch, and I've had enough to drink that my brain is on autopilot because I lean toward him as well—

And then Carlina spills her drink across the table.

I'm not exactly sure what time I got home last night, but Gemma told me I made a racket. I used my newfound journalism skills to piece together the end of the evening. The time my Uber dropped me off, according to the app, and the DoorDashed fast food I ordered give away more clues than the dry mouth I woke up with.

I'm not much of a drinker, and I let loose like this maybe once or twice a year. Usually, it's after a breakup or when I quit a job, but this was just a random Friday. And there's no breakup, because I'm not dating anyone for real, and Max was with me all night.

Flashes of memory hit me: Max grinning at me on stage. Max almost kissing me in the booth after he came back. Vee encouraging everyone to dance. Our shoes sticking slightly to the floor as we pumped our fists to songs from high school. Max's hands on my hips as I threw my arms in the air. Both of us scream-singing along with Lil Wayne, lyrics I hadn't thought about for years.

Last night *was* a good night. This morning, however, is not.

I trudge out to the kitchen after scrambling to find a T-shirt and shorts and find Gemma with a cup of cold water in one hand and two Advil in the other.

"Here," she says, shoving them into my hands.

"I adore you."

"Can your stomach handle coffee yet?" she asks, heading over to the counter. Apparently, the noise my stomach makes answers for me, because Gemma comes back with only one cup for herself. I flop onto the couch while Gemma curls into her corner, perching her coffee cup on her knee. "So, how was your night?" she asks, sounding like my mother the morning after I would sneak home after curfew.

Apparently, the groan I let out is not an acceptable answer.

"I got a fascinating series of text messages last night," she says, taking a delicate sip of her coffee.

"Oh no," I say, closing one eye. "What dumb shit did I send you from the bar?"

"There was a great video of you singing Paramore, as usual, but I also got a series of photographs from a dance floor? They're super blurry."

Okay, that's not so bad.

"I also got a few texts from Max."

"Max?"

Gemma grabs her phone from the arm of the couch, swipes it open, then passes it to me.

Hi.

Did Brooklyn get home safge

She needsadvil tomorrow

DUck

Fuck

I just wantto make sure sheok

I could go through the entiresong and dance of pretending it's not him, but I giggle a bit, imagining him getting frustrated at how his sentence structure and punctuation went to shit in the back seat of his ride home.

"That's Max," I say.

"Max, huh?"

"It's nothing. He does it all the time." I don't realize it until I say it, but Max is always checking in on me. He'll send a *text me when you get home* message, even if we've only had breakfast at the diner.

"Hmm," Gemma says, the sound more of a snort.

"It's *nothing*," I say, even though I want it to mean everything. Max probably makes sure that his dentist is flossing. It's just who he is.

"It's good to see you making work friends," Gemma says, subtly switching the subject.

"I mean, I'm always friendly."

"Friendly isn't the same as having friends," she says. "You've been pretty solitary, except for me, over the past few years. It's nice to see you going out again." Gemma's right, as usual. I used to go out all the time. I used to chat with coworkers on the weekends and over coffee. But then work shifted to remote and I didn't maintain those friendships. I guess they were friendships of convenience more than anything. Our biggest commonality was that we worked in the same office for forty-plus hours a week.

I think about Vee and Carlina and even a few other people I've started taking lunch with. A few of them fall into the coworker category, but I can't imagine not having Carlina sass me regularly or having Vee tell me about their latest hiking adventures.

And I don't even want to think about not seeing Max.

Luckily, I'm saved by the sound of my phone ringing in my bedroom. I stand up from the couch quickly, swallow a wave of nausea, then hustle to my room, where I have to rifle through my blankets to find the damn thing. I've got a missed call from Max, along with a series of text messages.

Brooklyn, how are you feeling this morning?
I'm glad you got home safe.
Do you want to get breakfast?
Okay, maybe not breakfast because it's late.
Lunch?

"Grinning at your phone?" Gemma asks, leaning against my doorframe.

"This is a private space," I respond.

"Psh." She waves a hand. "Is that Max?"

I nod.

"Good." She smiles. "I hate his sister, but I like him for you."

Chapter 15

Annoyingly, nothing happens at work over the next couple of days, with the exception of my hangover lasting forty-eight hours. I see Aron occasionally in the hallways, always with a cell phone pressed to his ear and a frustrated expression on his face. The marketing department produces materials, gets feedback, makes adjustments. Wash, rinse, repeat. I head home to Gemma and *The Bachelor* on Thursday, sending Max a text with an update that there is no update.

Max: That is frustrating, but that's journalism. Hurry up and wait!

I'm ready to slide my phone back into my pocket and wait to text him until something finally happens at work, but I get an idea. We have an event in a few days, the annual company party, and Max and I really need to convince everyone at work that we're a couple. The only time I've spoken to Aron recently was the time he asked me about Max, and the flare of jealousy on his face was enough to motivate me.

Brooklyn: What are you doing tomorrow night?

Max: I have a Shabbat dinner with some friends.

I make a mental note to google what *Shabbat* is. I feel like I'm constantly learning about Jewish holidays, so I assume it's one of those.

Brooklyn: Saturday night?

Max: Free. Why? Is there a work event?

Brooklyn: Kind of. We should go on a date.

I can feel his fingers preparing to type a reminder that we can't date for real. The day after The Kiss, Max sent me a few articles about journalistic ethics and added a few about the unfair expectations placed on female and nonbinary journalists to underline his point. I didn't need convincing after he told me it was something he wasn't comfortable with, but it definitely caused me to rethink my evening fantasy in the shower. So I clarify.

Brooklyn: Not a real date. But a date in a public place to get used to being around each other.

Brooklyn: As a fake couple.

Brooklyn: And to get to know each other better.

Brooklyn: For our backstory.

I'm verging on *she doth protest too much* territory when Max responds.

Max: Brilliant. I'm free after 11 am.

Brooklyn: Great. Meet me here.

I send him the address for the skating rink. Not only is it something I find fun, but there is nothing less sexy than being surrounded by high schoolers on dates while bored college kids home for break staff the rink in dollar store Santa hats. Plus, Max falling on his ass—as most people do when they start skating again as an adult—will tamp down both of our libidos.

I know from personal experience.

I've gone ice skating a few times, usually on dates that go nowhere or when a friend from someplace cold decides they want to remember why they pay so much money to sit in traffic on the 405. I'm not bad, but I'm not good, and I can wobble myself around the rink in a fair manner. I also imagine that it's going to be a winter wonderland. I've never seen a white Christmas, unless you count the one year my stepdad drove us out to the mountains to see the half inch of snow on the ground, but I like the imagery of it.

I haven't been able to explain to Max yet that my love of Christmas isn't about the holiday. I don't give a shit about gift giving or peppermint (though I do confess a love of eggnog). I like the idea that the entire season feels cozy. Simple. Warm. I imagine sitting in front of a fire, wearing pajamas that match my boyfriend's, sipping hot chocolate and watching *It's A Wonderful Life*.

That's what Christmas is about.

I get to the skating rink on time, hoping I've beaten Max here. I quickly pay for my admission and skate rental and pull out the high socks I brought to put over my black leggings. They're red and they're run through with a sparkly thread, with tiny candy canes running up and down the side. I text Max to let him know that I've arrived and lace up my skates. I'm doing the awkward shuffle on the rubber covering of the floor to the rink when I hear my name.

"Brooklyn!" Max is at the door, his glasses fogging from the change in temperature from outside to the rink. I give him a small wave to acknowledge him and curse the fact that he's seen me at the least graceful part of skating.

I'm annoyed; I wanted to be on the ice already, gliding around like some kind of Ice Skater Barbie. I wanted him to get that slightly glazed look on his face, like he looked at me at the diner. I'm worried that I'll never see that again, not after The Kiss.

Max comes over, and I notice that he's carrying an oddly shaped bag. It's shocking that I've noticed the bag before *him*. He's traded in his normal look—the button-up and chinos that have me suspecting he chooses his outfit based on asking an AI program to create a journalist. Today, he's wearing a long-sleeved gray moisture-wicking shirt with his thumb poking through holes at the wrists paired with dark blue joggers that reveal slightly more than his khakis do.

I'm still standing there, knees wobbling like a drunk baby deer, as Max pulls out a pair of black figure skates.

"You skate?" I sputter as all my plans of connecting over our shared falls fly out the window.

"A bit," he replies nonchalantly.

"You didn't tell me!"

"You didn't ask." He smirks at me as he laces up one boot.

It's impossible for Max to not be in journalist mode, which I'm starting to learn means taking things literally when it benefits him. Trying to find loopholes around him reminds me of trying to solve a puzzle cube in elementary school. I usually gave up and tried to just snap the plastic.

"Come on, Brooklyn. Let's begin this date." He steps past me and onto the ice, and my annoyance grows.

Maybe it's some kind of horrible stereotype I have in my head, or maybe I didn't think that men who wore Bass shoes in their thirties were athletic, but I didn't imagine that Max would be good at skating. From the way he swiftly crosses one skate over the other, though, it's evident that he's been doing this a long time, maybe since childhood. I figured he spent his childhood evenings at the library. Chess club. Practicing for the national spelling bee or geography bowl. He doesn't even seem to skate across the ice, but glides.

He's like fucking Nancy Kerrigan out there.

He laps the rink one more time and then flips around and does a lap backward. On the next lap, he does a stupid little jump, then skates over to me and comes to a perfect stop an inch away from where I'm standing, mouth open.

This explains his ass.

"I took skating lessons for ten years. It started because I had an enormous crush on Sasha Cohen, and my mom told me I needed to do something athletic. I'm not a team sports person"—at least I got that right—"and this was a way to keep my mind clear. I kept up a membership through college and beyond. I like to go to the rink a few times a month, especially when I'm stuck on a story."

"Oh," I say. "Would have been good to know. I would have chosen something that we're equally bad at."

"Why, when I get to see this look on your face?" Max gives me a pointed up and down look, and I feel my face flush despite the cool air. "Come on, let's date."

I step onto the ice, gripping the boards on the side of the rink. I know I can do this, but now I have something to prove. I focus on how I can make my body look graceful, to bend my knees and let my skates do what I know they can do. So, of course, I promptly feel my feet slide from underneath me and stumble. My knees hit the ice, and my hands grip the wall.

"Shit, fuck," I swear, feeling more like one of the Three Stooges than an ice princess.

"Brook," he says, the nickname effortlessly slipping past his lips. He skates over and reaches out. I pry my fingers from their death grip on the wall and reach one out. "Both," he commands.

So I grab his hands, and he pulls me up with an unexpected strength.

His hands are soft.

Max is full of surprises today.

"Just push off," he says, his voice dropping low.

"I know how to skate," I say through gritted teeth. I bristle when people tell me what to do.

"All right," to his credit, Max just continues to provide enough help to allow me to stand up. I take a tentative push, but he doesn't let go, and I don't either. He's just as comfortable skating backwards as he is forward. We make a tentative circle around the rink so I can get my legs underneath me.

"You can let go," I say. I feel comfortable enough that I can skate on my own.

"Nah," Max says. "We have to learn to be natural around each other. Couples hold hands, right?"

"Allegedly," I respond.

Max rolls his eyes and continues to lead me around the rink.

"All right, so. Rapid-fire questions." I shrug my shoulders and make a big production of rolling my eyes and sighing. When Max fixes me with a sharp glance, I roll my eyes again.

"What?" I ask. "I'm learning from the best. You roll your eyes, like, fifteen times an hour."

"Only when I'm around you." He rolls his eyes, and I raise my eyebrows, earning me a begrudging chuckle out of Max. My heart leaps, and I feel a sense of pride. I love bringing joy and humor to situations, but making this curmudgeonly man laugh is an extra challenge.

"All right, ask me questions like we're twins who were separated at birth and we're learning about each other's grandparents." He laughs afterwards, a healthy chuckle that has my knees weak again.

"College?" I ask.

"Northwestern. You?"

"UCLA."

CORPORATE MANDATED HOLIDAY ROMANCE 113

His turn. "Favorite food?"

"Street tacos. You?"

"Gyros."

My turn to ask a question. "Favorite color?"

"Light blue. You?"

"Dark purple." We're still moving around the ice, and I'm racking my brain, trying to think of things I've known about past boyfriends.

Max gives me a grin, and the way it lights up his entire face shocks me. It's not sarcastic or skeptical, but something else that causes his eyes to sparkle like the tinsel on trees in the old-timey movies. I let out a tiny gasp, and Max's eyes flit down to my lips. And just like that—

He catches an edge and falls down. And since he's still holding my hands because of his stubborn insistence that we should practice, he pulls me down with him. I land with an *oof*, my elbow on his stomach and our legs tangled together.

"Well, at least we have this PDA thing down," I joke. Max laughs, his breath against my cheek, then moves himself underneath me. I have to immediately shut down the image of how I'd love to have him under me in other ways, how we almost found ourselves there a few days ago.

Max grumbles something about how my knee is too close to an essential part, and I roll off him. The shock of the coolness of the ice on my knee brings me back to the reality of this situation.

This is bigger than us.

This is about exposing Aron for all the shit he's done.

This is about trying to make the future slightly better.

I need to keep it in my pants.

Which gets harder when Max gets up and adjusts himself with a wince, then a grin.

"Come on, Brook." He giggles—*giggles*—and we glide around the rink for another forty-five minutes until my ankles protest that I need a break. We hobble over to a table, and Max then heads to the snack bar. He comes back with an absurd amount of candy, explaining it away by telling me he doesn't know my favorite kind yet. He also brought nachos, which I'm grateful for.

I pick up a chocolate bar, and Max grabs a long, green package.

"I love chocolate of all kinds," I say. "How boring."

"Not boring. Classic."

My turn to roll my eyes again. "Hit me with another question, Mr. Reporter."

"What kind of underwear do you prefer?" he asks, pulling a sour straw through his teeth. The end in his mouth snaps off, and he chews thoughtfully as I process his question.

"What...kind...of," I sputter, blushing. "How dare you?"

"What?" He bites off another bit of the sour straw. Green apple. "It's something that a boyfriend would know. Unless you don't wear any at all, which is certainly a choice."

My mind flashes back to that night on the couch, the hint of a waistband peeking out when his shirt rode up. The way he didn't feel bulky underneath me, like boxers were shoved into pants.

"Brooklyn!" he cries out. "I'm growing old over here, waiting for you to answer."

"Fine!" I look down at my nachos. The cheese is starting to coagulate on the top. I skim off the layer with a chip and add a jalapeño. "The hipster ones that kind of show off my ass." I feel myself blushing. "Thongs if I'm wearing leggings. One time, none. I was on a date, and I wanted to try to be sexy." I shove the chip, cheese, and jalapeño into my mouth and immediately bite into a seed. The searing burn on my tongue is nothing compared to the blaze across my cheeks and the warmth between my legs.

Max looks at me, then ducks his head under the table. He comes back up and nods with a half smile on his face.

"What?" I ask, gulping down my soda.

"You're wearing leggings today," he replies.

"So?"

"Thong." He pumps his eyebrows once, and I purse my lips. Two can play at this game.

"Okay, well, what about you?"

"Standard issue Costco boxer briefs." He's unflappable in an interview. I have a strange desire to watch him *be* a journalist. Not this farce we're playing at, but tucked into the corner of a coffee shop, a recorder on the table as he grills a source for a story. In a press conference for a politician, asking the question everyone is thinking but no one has the courage to ask.

"Bo-ring," I snort.

"I'm full of surprises in other ways," he says.

Instantly, I'm on the back foot again. I stick my finger in the nacho cheese and lick it off. His eyes follow the movement, so maybe I hollow my cheeks out a bit more than is necessary.

Maybe.

The conversation maneuvers through stories from our youth, broken bones, and first crushes. He tells me about the DJ at his bar mitzvah, and I share about the first homecoming dance I went to and how I was so nervous I threw up beforehand.

As I head back to my car, Max shouts after me. "What are you doing next Friday?"

"Nothing. Fridays are when I start catching up on shitty reality television and rot my brain."

He blushes slightly, kicks at a pebble in the dirt. "Do you want to come over to my house for Shabbat dinner? A group of us get together. We swap who hosts every week, and it's my turn."

"Shabbat," I respond.

"Yeah, it's a—"

"Weekly Jewish dinner," I say proudly. "It starts at sunset, right?" Max nods, open-mouthed. Adopting his signature coy smirk, I continue, "I do have Google, you know. There are a fair number of Judaism 101 websites."

"But why did you—" He lets the end of the question linger in the dry air between us. It's the familiar beginning of questions I've asked myself a dozen times.

Why did you research this?

Why did you agree to help me with the story?

Why did you look at me like you wanted to kiss me?

I settle for the easiest question to answer. "You're helping me. I figured I could learn a bit about things that are important to you."

"Thank you," he says quietly.

"It's nothing."

"It's not nothing," he says, with that force in his voice that means he doesn't want to argue at all. There's emotion and history under what he's saying, but I'm too afraid to investigate it.

"Well, you're welcome. I'll see you at sunset on Friday." With a wave, I head to my car and pull up a podcast episode on Shabbat etiquette.

Chapter 16

By some miracle of Los Angeles traffic gods, I'm actually on time to Max's apartment. I didn't have to send a frantic text during slow down traffic that Max would chide me for. I have a trusty bottle of discount wine and something that I baked, because bringing homemade things is a nice thing to do. For a friend. I listened to a bunch of podcasts and did some googling, but the best advice I was able to glean was to just show up and be a good guest.

But these are Max's friends. I'm getting a peek into his real-life existence. He's reaching out. I don't want to just be a good guest. I want to be the best damn Gentile ever invited to a Shabbat in Los Angles. Honestly, it feels like it's an impossible bar to reach, but that's kind of how my life has been over the past month. Reaching for something that might not even be attainable.

As if to answer the unspoken question, Max opens the door. "You're on time?" is his greeting.

"Shabbat Shalom to you as well." I smirk back, and he grins, a full-on Max-not-in-journalism-mode grin. I take stock of how he looks here. I'm used to seeing Max at home, what with our late-night planning and preparation sessions that usually end up with Max scoffing and rolling his eyes through another animated Christmas special. Two evenings ago, it was Max asking me why all of Rudolph's friends were such assholes and then going on a small rant about the way Santa took advantage of his labor. I swear, by the end of the evening, he was about to start Reindeer Local 1.

His shoulders are relaxed. He holds a wooden spoon in his left hand, and the sleeves of his long-sleeved T-shirt are scrunched up. I hear chatter behind him and look around to see three other people seated around a folding card table like I used for lemonade stands in the summer when I was a kid.

"Let me introduce you to everyone," he says, smiling again, and I follow him in, the straps of the cotton bag starting to cut into my shoulders.

"It smells amazing," I compliment, which causes the tips of Max's ears to go a bit pink.

"It's nothing," he says. "I am the only son of a Jewish mother, so I spent a lot of time in the kitchen growing up. A lot of talk about how I had to make sure I could cook for my future wife." He lets out a small giggle.

"Don't let him lie to you," comes a voice from the card table. "He always shows off for Shabbat, even though we're supposed to be a humble people."

"Must be nice to freelance so you can spend the entire day making challah, you know," says a tall Asian woman who is playing with her phone.

"Don't listen to Mai," the first man, who has a mustache and tan skin, says, "She's just bitter she's still helping high schoolers with their feelings."

I make an inadvertent noise. Teaching scares the hell out of me.

"Yeah, that's about right," Mai says. "I'm a school psychologist. And I'm Mai." She puts her phone down and fixes Max with a shaming glare. "You are a terrible host, Maxim." The way she says it—*Max-eem*—makes me realize that she's not just making a joke.

"Wait," I say, turning to Max. "That's your name?"

"Yes," he says, turning even redder. "My parents went *really* Russian. My sister's full name is Galina. Galina and Maxim—as if being Jewish in Indiana wasn't rough enough, we then had kids constantly making Boris and Natasha jokes."

I swallow my urge to apologize for the fact that kids were assholes to him. If there's one thing I've learned from Max, it's that constantly apologizing for someone else's behavior is not helpful at all. "Well, Maxim," I try to mimic the way Mai says it. "I'm still Brooklyn."

"*This* is Brooklyn?" the third member of the table crew, a short man with an accent I can't place, says. "Oh, well, *bonjour* and *shalom* to the mystery woman we've heard so much about."

"I'm sure it's all complaints," I hedge.

"Yeah, but complaining about someone is Max's love language," the man with the mustache says. "I'm Luis, and when Max met me for the first time, he apparently told his sister that I was so full of myself he was sure my head would burst." He smiles at Max. "I felt the same as him. We've been best friends ever since."

"When was that?" I ask.

"Tenth grade," Max says, laughing. "I had just moved to California, and Luis was the only other Jew in my class. Mai and I met in college at the Hillel at Northwestern—that's a Jewish campus organization—and Henri started dating Luis three weeks before COVID lockdowns, so the four of us bubbled together."

"It's how I snagged this one," Henri says, pressing a kiss to Luis's hand. "He couldn't escape me for *months*."

"So, are you all..." I let the end of the question hang in the middle of the table, not sure if there's an appropriate way to ask if everyone here is Jewish or if they were also invited by a friend. "Let me rephrase," I say, smiling into my glass. "Is anyone else a token Gentile?"

Polite giggles burst out around the table, and I'm most heartened by the way Max gives a genuine laugh. I've learned how to pick them out—he's got a terse laugh when he's in public, a frustrated laugh he often gives me when we're brainstorming, and, the rarest one of all, a higher-pitched chuckle that means he's actually found something funny.

"We're all Jewish, yeah," Mai says. "And yes, before you ask, Jewish is not a race. It's a religious and cultural identity, so Jews can be any color under the sun. When people say they're Jewish, believe them." She sounds exhausted, like she's used to having to defend her identity.

"Cool. Sorry?" I say, feeling like I've made a small misstep but recovered.

Luis just laughs. "We usually take turns inviting friends," he explains. "Some people come back, some don't." He looks at Henri.

"Though," Mai says, looking pointedly at Max, "it's been a while since Max has invited a friend." She pours a glass of wine for herself. "How do you know each other?"

"His sister dated my roommate," I explain, remembering that the best lie is the closest to the truth. Not wanting to explain any more, I heave the bag off my shoulder. "Is there some place I can drop this off?"

"Oh, shit. Yeah, of course," Max says, and I follow him into the kitchen. It smells even better in here, savory with spices I know I've tasted but couldn't name.

"What are you making?"

"My standard Shabbat dinner," he says. "Challah—" He points to the braided loaf of bread that looks like it came from an Instagram ad. "And roasted chicken and potatoes with za'atar and salad." He takes the bag from me, pulling out a bottle of red wine and a pumpkin pie.

I cringe. "I know it's not necessarily Jewish, but a lot of the articles I read talked about the importance of seasonal food and a good dessert, and pumpkin pie is my favorite and—"

He lifts the cling wrap and gives the pie a tentative sniff. "Did you make this yourself?"

"Yeah, but it's been years since I've baked one, so if the crust is soggy or you don't like the spices, I can DoorDash us some ice cream or something."

"Brooklyn." He smiles at me, that genuine smile that has me believing that not everything is fake. "I think there is a truth universally acknowledged that everyone, regardless of culture, loves pumpkin pie spice."

The conversation is stilted at first, in the way that meeting new people always takes a bit to get used to. However, eventually, there are commonalities. Henri did his graduate work at UCLA, so we chat about campus and the changes we've seen in that area, and Mai and I find out that we both share an affinity for Bravo reality TV.

"See? I knew I liked her!" Mai shouts, fanning her cheeks after she finishes a glass of wine. She looks at me, giving a sly grin. "Want to go to that one restaurant that was the subject of the last scandal?" I nod, and Mai holds her hand out for my phone so we can swap numbers.

"My roommate and I watch every Thursday night," I say, taking a jump into the unknown. Or, at the very least, the unknown for the past three years. "You should come over." My half a glass of wine has clearly taken residence in my blood, because I throw Max a *look* and add, "I can promise you won't have to listen to anyone complain about the ethics of reality TV."

"Listen, the rise of reality television coincides with writer's strikes—" Max begins.

"Boo!" Luis says. "No one here is crossing a picket line, and *we know*. We just like to live in the drama for a little bit. Not all of us can be super-secret journalists." He rolls his eyes, and Henri laughs.

"Do you know anything about his current story?" Henri asks. "He's being very cagey with us. Usually, we get all the details each week."

"Me? Oh, no," I say, hoping that my white lies have been more convincing recently. "Plus, I usually tune out when he gets to rambling." Everyone chuckles, and Max gives me a small smile.

I like that it's a secret between us. Under the table, I feel Max's hand on my thigh. He gives a squeeze, a reminder that I did good, and it's something that stays between us.

Dinner turns into dessert, and dessert turns into everyone crowding onto Max's couch to take turns putting on different YouTube videos. By the end of the night, Luis and Mai are dancing.

My phone buzzes in my pocket, my reminder to go home and sleep like a responsible adult. I start to help clean up but get shooed away by the collective. They tell me that first-time guests don't clean, but I better pull my weight when I come back next time.

I hope there's a next time.

"I'll walk you out to your car," Max says, pointedly ignoring the suggestive stares and throat clearing from Luis, Henri, and Mai. Henri gives me a kind wave goodbye, and Mai mouths, *text me*. Then I leave with a warm, fuzzy feeling popping in my chest. Max walks me down and out onto the street where my car was parked.

"Thank you for coming tonight, Brooklyn," he says, opening my car door like he's been transported from the 1930s. Though Max would probably say something about how the only people who would want to time travel to that era would be white, straight, Christian men. I hold the laugh inside.

"It was lovely," I respond genuinely. "You have such an amazing group of friends. Honestly, I'm jealous. I don't have that many friends."

Max gives me his classic *Max* stare. "That's not true. I'm a journalist, Brook. I look for the stories and the things people can't see that are often staring them in the face. Yeah, Gemma adores you—I think she hates me because of my association with Lina, but whatever—but Vee and Carlina are also your friends. Everyone tonight really liked you. You even have plans with Mai. And," he looks tentative for a second before continuing, "I like you. I'm really happy to have you as a friend, Brooklyn."

And while it's a compliment and I don't ignore the way that Max has pointed out that I do have friends, I can't help but feel disappointed by how he ended that sentence. We're friends and nothing more. That line has been drawn and fortified time after time, yet, stupidly, I still keep hoping that he'll put just a toe across it.

We stand there, my ass awkwardly in my car's open door, my arm on the inside handle like I'm going to close it. Neither of us is moving, the rush of traffic behind us the only noise now. A laugh trickles out from an open window.

"Good night. Text me when you get home," Max says, and swiftly kisses me on the cheek. I let out a tiny gasp and look up at him, but he's walking back into the house, hands in his pockets.

My cheek burns as I close the door.

There are more evenings and more preparations. We've started to draft the story in the evenings, sticking Post-it notes on a whiteboard in Max's apartment in the time that Christmas cookies are baking. Another morning at Norm's, Max taught me how to play dreidel, each of us using sugar packets and cups of cream as our items to bet. The day after, his laptop and notebook sat to the side while we engaged in a debate about religion and sexuality until looks from the table next to us reminded us that we were in public.

Us.

Us.

Us.

Chapter 17

"Hi," I say, being awkward as usual. Max has always made me feel self-conscious, but it's even worse now that I've seen how he relaxes around me, the manner in which we've started to tentatively stitch together the patches of the story we're writing.

Max decided to come over to my house tonight, so I threatened Gemma with every single torture I knew she hated—leaving her socks wet after the laundry and drying everything else, forgetting to refill the ice trays, filling the dishwasher but not running it. All the minute details you pick up on after living with someone for over half a decade.

I look around the apartment and awkwardly adjust a throw pillow that says *home is where the pussy is* that Gemma bought while high a few years ago. Will he be offended? Max barely swears unless he's talking about the inherent unfairness of the late-stage capitalist empire we exist in. Heading over, I check the fridge—sodas, seltzers, one bottle of wine that sits lonely in the back of the fridge. I don't drink that often, and red wine triggers Gemma's migraines, so that bottle sits, a reminder of when I thought I would understand wine and be able to talk about it.

One more thing in a long line of abandoned attempts to feel connected to something larger than myself.

Before I can grow annoyingly morose, I hear my phone vibrate on the counter.

Max: ▪

Me: I take that to mean you're here?

Max: I thought emojis communicated full sentences without the need to add more detail?

I can almost hear the sarcasm in his text message. I send back a quick middle finger emoji, grab my keys, and head down to let him in. He holds up dinner—two bagged salads that we'll dump into mixing bowls and eat like vegetarian cavemen for the evening.

"Oh!" I say. "That dill flavor is new?" I internally cringe, thinking how pathetic it is that a new flavor of premade lazy salad is on par with celebrity news.

Max grins back. "I know! It's mine, though." He follows me through the gate and up to our apartment. "But if you're nice to me, I'll let you have a bite to try."

A flash of something hot streaks through my body, followed by a cold echo. It's become harder and harder to separate this—the Max who is a flirt to everyone, including me, and the Max who leans into it because we're supposed to be a couple. I've known people like Max—coworkers who give you *that* kind of smile over the Keurig machine. Like Carlina, who can't help but flirt with every waiter she sees. It's so warm when they turn their attention to you, but chilly when the sun sets. I never really feel like Max is ignoring me or playing me for a fool, but it's, well...

It's like opening up the adoption website for the local shelter and seeing all the animals I can't have because of my lease. Something that makes me feel good but somehow makes me feel worse because there's a boundary.

"Any new information?" Max is asking from the kitchen. He emerges with two seltzers—lime for me and lemon for him—after putting our dinner away.

"Nah," I say, folding myself up on my usual place on the couch. "Same usual gossip. Aron has been out of the office this entire week, so any meetings he normally runs are being organized by Zane."

Max pulls a face. "What a name."

"Right? But I was able to pull the last seven years of quarterly reports—I told Carlina I was curious about the evolution of the style guide for internal publications." She gave me a suspicious look, lovingly called me a brown-nosing overachiever, then sent a link to them. It came from her personal email, sent to mine. A fact that would have seemed a quirk of technology a month ago, but now is a detail I pick up on.

"You're not the only one who knows that things are fishy," Max comments after I tell him. "You're just the only one with enough chutzpah to do anything about it." Max opens up his laptop, scrolls through the quarterly reports. He's talking to himself about how we can compare the reported amount of trash exported to China pre- and post-ban to the number of financial reports I managed to snap photos of. We think—we hope?—that Aron and ConservTech have continued to sell recycling to third parties who, in reality, are just dumping it into the ocean.

Meanwhile, I'm engaged with a mini project of my own. Pulling out my phone, I quickly google *chutzpah*, taking two attempts to spell it.

Hootspa - which autocorrects to *foot spa*

Hutzpah - which directs me to the proper definition.

Chutzpah (adj.) - uncommon boldness

We work together for a bit, Max using his knowledge of the web of the internet to find out information on Aron while I send a few questioning texts to friends I've made from work. Max reminds me to get everything in writing, so I screenshot long replies and ask if my coworkers are comfortable letting me save their thoughts. Not for the first time, I think that some of them know what I'm up to, but they've adopted a "don't ask, don't tell" policy. Scratch the surface of anyone who's been at ConservTech for longer than three months, and it seems they have a story.

Or a memo they forwarded to their personal email *just in case*.

Or a photograph that they snapped of a document and saved *just in case*.

And we've been collecting them and piecing together two major stories. Max has been taking lead on the fact that it appears as if Aron, through the guise of ConservTech, takes garbage contracts from small governments and promises a more sustainable and cheaper waste disposal. Unsurprisingly, it's not cheaper for the local governments, and it appears as if the recycling is just being dumped somewhere in the Pacific Ocean.

For me, I've been tying together the stories of women who have been...well, the euphemism in reports is "approached" by Aron and offered "unique job opportunities," but I've been a woman for thirty-five years and know what that means. As Vee and Carlina told me, there is a record of large bank transfers to private citizens, along with NDAs that were filed by the company's lawyers at roughly a week before the financial transfer. Max has been giving me readings from legal and financial writers about the consequences of breaking NDAs with the hope that I can get someone to agree to go on the record. It

CORPORATE MANDATED HOLIDAY ROMANCE 129

still hasn't happened, though I have a potential lead that I feel good about.

About an hour in, Max flops onto the couch. I'm wearing a hoodie and a set of old running shorts, and I feel the heat of his body next to mine. He looks up at me, a piece of hair falling across his eyes. I clench my fist so I don't move it away. "Put on a movie," he says, a demand with no heat behind it. "Something that will give me hope."

I mentally scan a list of films, and then I think about one that, while a Christmas film, I think Max will like. A movie that was always on the television at some point in December, one that, while morbid, always gave me hope.

"Have you ever seen *It's a Wonderful Life*?"

Max groans. "No movie that's about the true meaning of Christmas, please."

I smirk, knowing I can get him riled up. "What if I told you that this movie involved an everyday guy fighting against an evil banker?"

As I predicted, that piques his interest. But, as is Max, he looks at me skeptically over the frames of his glasses. "You made that plot up."

A few clicks of my phone, and the movie is ready to begin. "Though," I say thoughtfully, "you should know that this movie does involve a character with thoughts of suicide. Is that okay?"

Max nods, then places his hand on my arm. "Thanks for checking." I press play and give Max a quick overview of the characters and their relationships.

Gemma pokes her head out of her bedroom when she hears the television. "I'm gonna marry you one day, George Bailey," she quotes. Then she attempts an absolutely horrendous Jimmy Stewart impression.

Gemma leaves for an event or a date early on, probably to avoid my annual rant about how this entire movie is really Uncle Jimmy's fault. Though, looking at Max, I consider that it's probably the fault of unregulated banking, and Uncle Jimmy is a symptom of it all.

It's my first time watching a movie with Max, and he's so *Max* about it.

"Wait, wait, wait." He grabs the remote from next to me, his fingers grazing my bare thigh. "In this no George Bailey future, the worst thing that can happen to her is that she's a bespectacled librarian?" I snort out a laugh, not even bothering to make fun of the fact that Max is a man who uses *bespectacled* in normal conversation.

I can tell that Max is enjoying the movie because he talks less and less as it progresses. Finally, the entire cast sings, and Zuzu taps the bell, causing my nose to sting. It always gets me, the way George Bailey was so close to losing everything but was able to save the town and his family. I look over at Max, whose eyes are red rimmed as well. His elbows are on his knees and he's leaning forward to get closer to the celebration on screen.

"Does that mean Clarence got his wings?" he asks.

I nod, then add, "George Bailey was a guy with a whole lot of *chutzpah*."

The grin Max sends me sets off enough bells in my chest to give an entire battalion of angels their wings.

Chapter 18

THE HOLIDAY PARTY IS accompanied by an open bar, which means that enough wine has been consumed to cause people to break out of their tiny pockets of departments and plus-ones and mingle. I don't think I've talked to this many people since the first day, and I've mostly stuck to the marketing department and their friends since. Max is chatting to Carlina's boyfriend about the best times to visit the museums in town, and I can hear Vee complaining about traffic. Things feel, well, *normal*. I take another sip of eggnog, the dusting of cinnamon on top causing my nose to wrinkle.

"Here," Max says, pulling a handkerchief from his pocket in the nick of time as I suppress a tiny sneeze.

"Thanks," I say. I awkwardly hold the piece of fabric in my hand. "Do you, uh, want this back? I did wipe my nose on it after all."

"You can keep it," he says, laughing. "I've got spares in my bag."

I roll my eyes and stick it in the pocket of my jumpsuit. I run my fingers over the hem, feel the bumps of a monogram on one corner. Of course he has a monogrammed hankie. Somehow, Max has the smirk of a fourteen-year-old and the habits of an eighty-one-year-old, all wrapped up in a midthirties body. It's a combination that always has me on my toes. I never know what he'll come up with next. As if to prove the point to the part of my brain that can't shut off my attraction to him, I hear him add a *nice* during the raffle ticket drawing when the number sixty-nine is called.

"What are they even auctioning off?" he asks, sliding back next to me, causing the hair on my arms to stand straight at attention. It's loud in the room, so I have to focus on his mouth to understand what he's saying, and if I lean a bit closer to him, it's only to ensure that he hears me as well, too.

"A bunch of random holiday things," I say. "There was a list in the email, but nothing looked too exciting, so I didn't pay attention to it." I fish around in my other pocket and pull out my ticket. "I'm ready to win, though."

"Eyes on the bigger prize," he says, looking over toward the corridor that leads to the CFO's office. I know in my gut that we'll get into that office and we'll be able to find the final piece of what we need. We just need a distraction to get there.

"Do we want to head over now?" I ask as everyone has turned their attention to where the CFO is announcing the winners of the raffle with a flourish. While Aron is at least believable as someone who isn't a complete piece of shit, CFO is every bit the grumpy, closed-off stereotype that I imagine lives in every high-rise in downtown Los Angeles, like a *Batman* villain or the guy with the cat from *Inspector Gadget*.

"No!" Max looks offended at me. "What if we win the raffle?" I've got no words for this, no witty comeback, so I sit next to him, running my fingers over the soft fabric of his handkerchief in my pocket.

"Next up," CFO announces, grimacing through the list of items he has to raffle off before he can slink back into his office, "A Chri—er, um, a holiday ham!" He rolls the bingo counter once, then pulls out a token. "Sixty-six!"

"That's me," says a woman I vaguely recognize from internal data analytics, one of the few who actually prefers to come to the marketing department to chat about what she wants rather than just sending an email that is more numbers than words I know. Rachel, I think her name is.

"Come on up and get your prize," Zane says, looking absolutely ridiculous as he holds up an entire frozen honey ham.

"No," says Rachel, and the crowd goes silent. The only sounds are a few gasps and the gulp of alcohol. I haven't been at ConservTech long, but I do know that Aron and Zane aren't told no very often, a message I heard loud and clear the first time I tried to reschedule one of Aron's check-ins. I peek around Max to see Rachel. She's wearing a deep blue velvet dress that hugs her curves in phenomenal ways. Her arms are crossed over her chest, and she's wearing a defiant look on her face that reminds me of the time I tried to convince Max that *Die Hard* was a Christmas classic.

"Why?" Zane says, stunned that someone would publicly question him.

"I keep kosher," she says. "I can't eat that." Zane sputters, then he digs around on the table and pulls out a gift certificate to some fancy restaurant in Los Feliz and waves it in the air.

"Do you want this?"

"I guess," Rachel says, smirking as she sashays up to the podium to take her prize. I can feel Max laughing next to me, and I'm all of a sudden jealous of Rachel. This is the type of woman he should be with—loud, outspoken, confident, brilliant. Determined to do her career her way.

Jewish.

Not me. Not a shiksa who is so afraid to cause conflict that she has taken to hiding and sneaking around to get things done. Not the kind of woman who gave up her passionate dream of protecting the environment to mess around with font kerning for social media posts instead.

"I'll introduce you to her," I say, my feet moving before I can think twice. Because if I can't have Max—and I can't—then someone amazing deserves him. He deserves to have someone amazing, too.

"Rachel?" I ask her. She's sipping a clear beverage and looking distastefully at the envelope the gift card came in.

"Hey, Brooklyn," she says. She holds up the card, which has a family of snowmen on it. "This is bullshit."

"Because it's hinting at Christmas or because it's a stereotypical nuclear family?" Max asks, piping in.

"Yes," Rachel says, smiling at him. Something hot and acidic burbles in my stomach, and I push it down, reminding myself that I'm here to set Max up. Even though the entire office thinks we're dating. At least he'll get a good rebound out of our fake breakup. "And you are?"

"Max Matuschansky," he says, extending his hand. Rachel shakes it.

"Rachel Gold," she says, then cringes. "Yeah, I know, I know." I don't know, but Max does, huffing out a polite chuckle, which I copy a second too late. She gives Max a once over, her eyes bouncing from the slightly tamed curls on top of his head down to his shiny leather shoes. I know, because it's the look I give him almost daily. "Are you related to Galina?" she finally asked.

"That's my sister!" Another reason they're perfect for each other.

"How is she?"

"Moved out to Colorado, helps run a bar. Happily miserable, as always." Max seems to remember I'm there and slides an arm around my waist. I resist the urge to preen. "How do you know Lina?"

"She dated my ex-girlfriend after I did. Neither of us talk to her anymore, but we became friends until we lost touch during COVID," Rachel explains, taking another sip of her drink. Max and Rachel continue talking, figuring out who they know in common, which is something that I've seen Max do with other Jewish people he's met throughout Los Angeles. Max told me it's something he does without thinking, but then he got philosophical and started talking about how it's a way to find community out here, knowing that he's always going to be a minority as a Jew in America.

I'm listening to Rachel and Max's conversation—now moving to complaining about their mothers—I really am. But my focus is on the way that Max's arm has tightened around my lower back, how his fingers have begun to brush up and down the curve of my hip. Just small movements—up and down, occasionally a small circle—so much that I miss when Rachel asks me a question. I only realize this when Max gives me a little pinch. Not to hurt, just to bring me back to the present moment.

"Huh?" I say eloquently. Internally cringing, I hold up my drink. "Sorry, whoever made the eggnog had a bit of a heavy hand."

"It's fine, my martini is mostly vodka that someone dipped an olive in," she laughs, and I immediately feel welcome and warm. I want to be her friend, but if she starts dating Max, that means I'll have to see them together all the time and—"How did you meet?"

"Us?" I squeak. Max chuckles next to me, squeezing my hip again.

"Brooklyn's roommate dated Lina, too," Max explains, a truth that holds the secret. "She had a question about a story I wrote, so we got breakfast." He looks at me, and a soft smile lights up his face, almost as if there is a wreath of Christmas lights above us. "She walked into the restaurant looking flustered and angry at the world, and I thought that I wanted to get to know this gorgeous woman better. Lucky for me, she's as smart as she is gorgeous. I was enraptured from the first breakfast."

"That's one way of putting it," I say, hoping that my laugh can drown out my pounding heart. "Mostly, I ate a giant breakfast while Max told me about the death of print journalism and how independent media is the one hope for a free press and a functioning democracy." Max has the audacity to look offended. I continue, my cheeks a bit warm, my attention still on that damn hand that hasn't moved more than an inch in the past few minutes. "Listen, at this point, I've heard that speech so much I could recite it in my sleep."

"You're lucky I don't talk in my sleep," Max says.

"Or maybe you do," I reply, wishing more than ever I actually could know. "And I just haven't told you yet."

"Are you keeping secrets from me?" he asks, his tone playful but with a serious undertone.

"No!" *Yes. I like you more than I should.* "Are you?" I wrinkle my nose at him.

"I don't lie to you, Brooklyn," he says, a refrain that's as common as his rants about shitty men with podcasts replacing trained journalists. I want to believe him, that everything he's said about me is true and not a part of this act. There has to be some bit of preservation for myself. I'm already going to lose my job and my income at the end of this. I can't have my heart broken, too.

"All right, lovebirds," Rachel says, smirking. "I get it. You're obnoxiously head over heels, and it's gross." She laughs into her martini. "Max, it was lovely to meet you. Brooklyn, I'll see you around the office. We need to stick together."

"We?" She's in a different department than me.

"Those of us who know what kind of bullshit is going on behind closed doors here." With that enigmatic statement, she's gone in a cloud of smirks and spicy perfume.

Chapter 19

"She's fun," I say to Max.

"If she hadn't already dated Lina, I'd be calling her to take the next flight here and booking a U-Haul," he replies. Even though Rachel's walked away and the raffle is wrapping up, Max still has his hand on me.

"What's next at these types of things, darling?" Max asks, pulling me around to face him, looping his arms around my waist.

"You don't have to." I wave between us.

"It's fine," he replies, almost tightening his hands more. "Keeps up the façade. Anyway, what's next?" I scrunch up my face and try to think back to my previous companies.

"Well, I've watched people get so drunk on a booze cruise that they try to swim in the Bay, and I watched a couple get into a huge fight on the Santa Monica Pier one year because of a misplaced piece of mistletoe. One time, there was a white elephant exchange where someone brought a bit of coke as the prize and no one would own up to it, but, like, seven designers almost came to blows looking for it at the end of the party." Max gives me a look like I snuck in after curfew.

"Not me! I don't fuck with that stuff," I explain.

"So, what you're saying is that most of these parties are excuses for people to act like idiots?"

"Yeah, but it's on the company's dime," I say.

"I'm sure Jesus would be so proud," he deadpans.

"I dunno. At better places I've worked, it's less of a *holiday* party"—I put the phrase in air quotes to let him know that I know what holiday they meant—"and more of a celebration that the year is over."

"Then why not just call it a New Year's party?"

"I don't know, Max," I say, exasperated. "I'm sorry I'm not as smart as you and don't think critically about every single aspect of contemporary American culture. I'm sorry that I've just gone along with things for my adult life and I'm just now untangling it all." I let go of him and pinch the bridge of my nose, take a breath deep into my belly.

"I didn't mean that," he says softly. I continue to walk away—away from the party and away from Max. I wish I could walk out into the bustle of Los Angeles at Christmastime. Between the tourists and the locals, I could get lost in the crowd and disappear from whatever I've made happen. But I don't, because there are still things I need to do here. So I weave my way through the crowd, grabbing a bottle of water and cursing the fact that I have to take a bit of single-use plastic as a cover right now. Heading vaguely toward my office, I turn into a storage closet, oddly comforted by the boxes of paper clips and reams of paper.

I only get to wallow in the dark by myself for about three breaths before a shadow darkens the sliver of light at the base of the door.

A quiet knock. "Brooklyn?"

"Nope," I say, sniffling just a bit.

"Brook, can I come in?"

"It's a storage closet, not a private bedroom," I quip.

The handle turns quietly, then the door snicks shut behind him. The closet is larger than any I've ever had to store clothes in, but the minute Max enters the space, it's imbued with his presence. The smell of newsprint and frankincense. Max, always a step ahead, turns around and presses the handle, locking the closet.

"Why can you even lock those closets?" I ask, trying to avoid the elephant in this tiny room—the fact that I ran away from him and he followed. "That seems like a fire hazard. You should probably contact the fire marshal and file an anonymous complaint and start a surprise investigation."

I expect him to try to comfort me, because it's obvious that I've been crying, but Max laughs. "You're thinking like a journalist," he says, pride evident in his voice.

"Oh joy," I say, no excitement in my voice. "So when I have to quit this job, I can join a dying field."

"Brooklyn," he says, my name coming out in a whisper. "Are you okay?"

"No!" I whisper-shout. "I am not okay, Max. This is *hard* on me. I'm not like you. This is new for me. At first it was fun, like *oh look at me, I'm a super spy*, but I'm struggling. I can't keep lying to my coworkers—they're my *friends*. I can't morally allow them to keep working for this company when I know we're about to do our damnedest to tank it. I won't be able to sleep at night if Vee or Carlina lose their jobs with no severance." I take a breath, and even more comes out. "I've been watching documentaries when I can't sleep. Whether it was Enron or Theranos or Pets.com, it's always the employees who get fucked when these companies go down. Even if Aron gets jail time, it'll be cushy. He'll pay a high-powered lawyer to get him sentenced to "time served" or community service, and the people who actually believed in the mission have to start again." Hot tears are running down my face, but I'm not sobbing. Rather, it's like all the frustration and anger I've been pushing down like a good WASP has come exploding out through the ducts in my eyes. "This is hard on me, Max. It's hard to pretend to be in a relationship when I'm not. It's hard to have what I actually want *right there* in front of me and not be able to have it, to hear the things you say to me and not believe they're real."

All Max responds with is "Brooklyn, I've never lied to you."

"I know you don't think of it as lying, Max," I say, frustrated and wiping the tears that have started to pool on my chin. "It's for the story, it's for the greater good, but I'm hitting the point where I can't listen to you tell me these things and hold my hand and not want something more. At this point, I might as well tattoo the words *it's not real* on my forehead so I get a constant reminder."

"No, Brooklyn." He takes my chin between his thumb and his forefinger and lifts my gaze to look at him. His face is intense, serious, and his eyes are scanning my face. "I. Don't. Lie. To. You."

And then he kisses me.

It's a different kiss than the ones we've had in front of my coworkers, which were nothing more than relatively chaste brushes of lips against my knuckles or my cheek. It's not even like the one we had on his couch the other week, even though that seems like a lifetime ago. This is something desperate, something hungry. There's nothing about the way that Max's lips take mine that I can write off as "for the story" or as a pity kiss, not when he's pressing me against the storage room door and his hands are gripping my torso hard enough to leave the best kind of bruises.

I'm not helping things, either, by grabbing his upper arms like he can save me from drowning and running my tongue over his lips until his meets mine. In seconds, it's officially progressed from a kiss to a full-on make-out. And I can't imagine that I've been the most professional employee over the past few weeks.

"Can I?" he asks, his hand crawling down my thigh until it reaches the edge of my dress.

"Yeah, please," I say, wanting to push him down to his knees so he's closer to where I want him. Or some kind of logic that will get his face between my legs sooner rather than later.

"Or I can?" he says, subtly picking up what I want so badly and beginning to lower his body.

And then we both freeze.

Because on the other side of the door, there are voices.

Voices that, quite literally, keep me up at night. Because it's Aron and Zane, joined by a third voice.

Max presses a finger against my lips, and even I know I'm at the moment to keep quiet, even though all I want is to pull that finger between my lips and suck.

I slip my phone out of my pocket and unlock it quickly. I start to take down notes while Max unlocks his own phone and starts to record. There's an angry conversation about a contract with the Altadena chamber of commerce and, if I'm not mistaken, just enough detail to confirm what Max has been tracing. Our eyes meet, only lit by the glow of our cell phones, and I see a spark of victory in Max's eyes.

We've got him.

We stay, me tapping away, and Max, still as a statue, until Zane and Aron storm away in a huff. Max taps once to end his recording, then presses a swift kiss to my cheek. I know I should be jumping for joy now that we've captured this slam-dunk piece of recording, but I start to feel a bit morose. Because finishing the story means that Max and I are finishing in this capacity.

"Wait a few minutes, then follow me," he says.

Chapter 20

I WAIT THE APPROPRIATE five minutes and walk out. I round the corner and adjust my skirt, catching both Vee and Carlina's eye.

"Nice," Carlina says, and Vee purses their lips.

"It wasn't—" I start to say, but it *was*. Unconsciously, a sly smile spreads across my face.

"Max told *us* to tell *you* that he's waiting downstairs," Vee adds. "Have a fun evening."

"I hope you get no sleep," Carlina adds.

"I hope you both have horrible hangovers." I smirk back. I follow Max to his car, and he drives me home, somehow finding every single opening in traffic to get downtown faster than I thought was humanly possible.

"Are those recordings legal?" I ask, the one fear I've had since we were in the closet tumbling out of my mouth.

"Remember that new hire paperwork you signed?"

I swallow. "I remember scrolling down and clicking *agree to all.*"

"You gave blanket consent to all recordings within the building." Max takes a deep breath. "I couldn't sleep one night so I read it and it caught my eye. I called a lawyer friend and he said its legally defensible for them." A beat. "And us." He's always seven steps ahead of me. "It feels like things are on our side," Max says, darting around a Tesla.

"I sure hope so." We tumble into the lobby and reach for the elevator call button at the same time, our fingers brushing. We've fallen into a routine—Max goes for his computer, while I grab the poster board that's grown to encompass dozens of Post-it notes that we've rearranged and taped back on a few times. A few minutes in, while I process my thoughts out loud and Max's fingers dance across the keys, I realize I haven't sat down since we arrived.

"This dress is so uncomfortable," I say, falling onto the couch. Max leaves the room without saying anything and comes back with a pair of basketball shorts and a sweatshirt for me.

"Here," he says, like it's a normal thing, like we're actually dating and I borrow his clothes all the time.

"Thanks," I mumble in response, heading down the hallway to change.

The evening is kind of a blur. We alternate between who types and who dictates, reading passages back and forth and figuring out how information fits into the narrative. I feel like one of those savants in a movie, able to see how chess pieces or math equations coalesce to unlock what we've been looking for. Max occasionally takes breaks to call editors he knows from his freelancing jobs, the ones who have taken small bits of what we've been putting out.

"Pizza?" he asks sometime around eleven.

"Please," I say, realizing I haven't eaten for hours. When it arrives, we eat quickly and the emotional toll of the evening crashes over me. I'm leaning against Max when his phone buzzes. I assume it's one of his freelancing jobs and not a potential girlfriend, but I still push down my initial impulse to look over his shoulder and read the screen. Max should know by this point that if anyone is opening a screen near me, I'm reading the text message.

He does know, because I noticed that during our second week together, he turned off the message preview on his phone. Which probably serves me right.

I'm only able to resist this impulse for about ten seconds. Because I'm resisting so much else: I'm resisting the urge to press my lips to that space on his jaw where a muscle jumps when he's stressed. I'm resisting the need to crawl across his lap and press my mouth to his, like that one night that feels like a lifetime ago. I'm resisting the instinct to lay it all out on the line, to let Max know that I genuinely like him as more than a friend.

And that I think he feels the same about me.

But another text message comes through just as I'm about to open my mouth. I look over Max's shoulder, but he turns away to read the message.

I feel and hear Max collapse into a shell of himself with disappointment. We've been rejected by most of the major West Coast newspapers. We've been waiting for a response from ProPublica, and Max had a good feeling about it because of a story of his they ran a few years ago and a former classmate who worked some beat.

That disappointment rattles through Max's bones and moves into my body. "They're not ready to run it," he says.

I feel it, too, the sensation that we're grasping at something just out of reach. I know we have enough for a full story. We have enough evidence and interviews (off the record) that any news organization could run a story. I've known that, somewhere in my gut, since I took that first photo, from the first time I sat down at that sticky diner table and came face to face with Max's cynical expression. That disappointment with a not-insignificant undercurrent of anger reminds me that

I have to keep resisting those impulses. Kissing Max is a temporary solution. Breaking this story and taking ConservTech and Aron and every asshole on his list of contacts down is a long-term step toward making the world better.

"Okay. What next?"

He laughs. "I like your optimism, Brook."

"What did they say? Was it an outright refusal?"

"No," Max says carefully. "They're putting it in the queue, beginning to fact check—"

I punch Max in the arm. "That's not a no! That's a vital step! And one that means they see some sort of validity in our story." Max looks at me, and I can see the gears turning in his mind.

I think back to what my stepdad told me the first time we all piled into the minivan and drove to the Grand Canyon. It was my first trip with my stepdad. What really stuck with me was the power of incremental change.

"Look, Brook," he said, chuckling a bit at the rhyme. "You see that tiny lil river down there?" I had to squint to make out the ribbon of blue at the base of the canyon that seemed to have been carved out by God. "That little river made this whole canyon."

"No way!"

"It did," my mom said. She took me by the hand, even though I was eleven and much too old for that, and directed me to the visitor center where a hands-on model took me through the various phases of the canyon. She bought me a Time-Life book about the Grand Canyon that I read until I threw up just across the Arizona-California border.

I want to point to all of our evidence now and adopt the same tone. Show Max that all the little photos and interviews we did have the potential to take it all down. "You see that bit of journalism? Those two made the whole story."

Max is silent, rotating his phone in his hand. It's the silence that lets me know how hard he's taking it. All I want to do is smooth a path for him. I can't kiss him and I can't bare my soul, so I turn to a safe question.

"Do you have a winter comfort movie?"

He turns to me, and my heart gives an extra *thump* when I catch sight of his red-rimmed eyes. I fix him with a faux-serious stare. "And I don't mean watching *Spotlight* and commenting on the ways in which Christian assumptions allowed that story to be squashed under the rug."

He gives a wet chuckle and takes a big breath. "You do listen."

"Not everything you say is boring," I respond. I nudge my shoulder against his. "So what is it? What makes you feel good?" As soon as that question is out of my mouth, I want to pull the words out of the air and shove them back into my throat.

Let me make you feel good.

"I don't have a favorite Christmas movie, though I did enjoy *It's a Wonderful Life*," he says. I breathe a sigh of relief. We're back to steady ground. "I think it's odd that your people think *The Sound of Music* should be played at this time of year."

"*Brown paper packages tied up with string,*" I sing.

Max winces. "Weird that the most popular movie involving World War II has nary a Jew in sight."

"Fair point. Are there Hanukkah movies?"

"I think Hallmark has put some out recently as a money grab in the same way that became strangely okay with gay couples when they realized we had money to spend." And there's my Max, the way he acknowledges progress with the understanding that money drives it all.

"My friend lives in Colorado and says there's a brewery there that hosts a public drinking game that goes along with Hallmark movies."

"My sister went to one of those, too. Spent the whole night catcalling the movies and ended up becoming best friends with the owner."

"*Eight Crazy Nights*?" I don't know where I pull that title from.

"Adam Sandler is a hero, but that movie isn't his best," Max responds.

"That's all I've got, unless you want to watch me cry at *Frosty the Snowman*."

Max turns to me and gives me that look, that side eye that means he's about to unleash a thousand questions and won't stop until I uncover something that I don't even realize. I swear, he's better than the therapist I went to after college. I roll my eyes and turn to him on the couch, take a sip of the red wine that we forgot about. "It's sad when he melts. All these little kids have just gotten a friend, and then he leaves them? I don't know if *Frosty* or *Puff the Magic Dragon* makes me cry more." I start to feel my eyes tingle just thinking about the blond girl with pigtails saying goodbye to the jolly snowman.

"He comes back every year," Max corrects. "Which is so up your alley it's ridiculous. A good friend who comes back every year to make the world better? That has Brooklyn Peters written all over it."

"Hey!" I say, taking his wineglass out of his hand and taking a sip of it just to claim some victory, and then I realize. "You've seen *Frosty*!"

"I grew up in Indiana, Brooklyn. You can't escape Christmas culture when you go to public school."

I'm a bit dumbfounded. "Then why did you let me spend the last few weeks teaching you all this stuff if you knew it?" I'm confused—I don't know whether to be angry or flattered or if I should just feel foolish.

"Because I knew the outlines of what was expected. Enough to follow and contribute to conversations throughout my life. But I couldn't have told you that there was a song about wanting a large mammal for a holiday gift or exactly who Saint Nicholas was." He looks down at his wineglass and takes a thoughtful swallow. "It's been nice to see it through the eyes of someone who doesn't instantly reject it."

"It's been nice to share my favorite and the most ridiculous parts of it." I remember the night we bonded over the fact that *Silver Bells* is essentially a carol to capitalism. I remember the night Max and I baked Christmas cookies, the way he focused so intently on making sure the Hershey Kiss was exactly in the middle of every cookie. "And you've taught me a lot, too. I didn't realize how much of Jewish culture and tradition was out there. Especially in California and Los Angeles."

"Well, it's not just that we control Hollywood," he jokes, and I swat his arm.

"There's so much," I begin.

He hooks a finger in the belt loop of my jeans. "Levi Strauss."

"Levi Strauss," I repeat.

"*Rugrats*," he says, interrupting my focus on the proximity of his hand to my hip. "Huh?"

"We may not have a holiday movie, but we have *A Rugrats Chanukah*." He's grinning when he says it, that grin that comes when he's talking about the importance of protecting sources or his favorite font and line spacing. Serious things he enjoys.

"Wait, *Rugrats*?" I slide back on the couch. Max's left hand is still resting on my hip; I can feel the tension in the denim from where his finger is still looped through. "Like Tommy Pickles?" Maybe talking about an animated show from over thirty years ago will help calm the fire in my blood. And the pulsing between my legs.

"Yeah." He sighs, a mix between a laugh and a noise I've taken to describing as "general existential angst coming out of his mouth." "Did you realize that the Pickleses were Jewish?"

"Not this again," I say, giggling partially because I'm exhausted and partially because I'm remembering the day Max went on about how certain office supplies were Jewish and others were Gentile. Apparently, most staplers are not Jewish, but quality metal Swingline Staplers are.

"No, really!" he says, turning on his television. "They're Jewish! There were episodes about Passover and Hanukkah, and they went to Temple and, well..." He takes a sip of water. "It wasn't weird, you know? Like these were babies on adventures and they just happened to also be Jewish. It wasn't like, *The Jewish Show* or anything. It was casual. Nice. Accepting." The TV turns on, and he navigates to the streaming app that currently has the rights to the show. "Plus, it taught all of my Indiana classmates how to say Hanukkah correctly."

"You strike me as a PBS Kid," I say, pulling my feet up on the couch.

"I mean, we did love watching *Antiques Roadshow*, but that was just because my bubbe was convinced that something she brought from Russia would be worth a lot of money someday. I think we have a doll that hides shot glasses under her dress?" Max chuckles, and I do, too.

"Okay, am I allowed to ask questions?"

"Grandpa Pickles explains it well," Max says, patting my hip. He doesn't move his hand as the familiar intro begins. I haven't watched an episode of this show in over two decades, probably longer, but I remember the dynamics as clear as day.

"Are all the characters Jewish?" I ask.

"No, we really only know about this family," he says, "But I did read somewhere that it's assumed that Mr. and Mrs. Pickles have an interfaith marriage."

"Interfaith?"

"Jewish and Gentile," he responds simply, and I do my damnedest to focus on the episode and learning about how the oil lasted, but in the back of my mind, I think about that.

Interfaith.

Am I religious? Not particularly, in the way that is common for millennials. We vaguely went to church growing up. Christmas and Easter were more about stockings and chocolate eggs. And family. Familiarity. Comfort.

A lot of what Max has explained about Judaism, a lot about what I've learned on my own, echoes the same themes. A sense of wanting to make the world better, of doing what's right for your community. I know there's more, because there's always more, but I want to learn.

The episode progresses, and I feel Max relax next to me. "Did you have a good Hanukkah this year?" I ask, pronouncing it the way Angelica does during the episode.

"It was lovely," he says, leaning a millimeter closer to me. "Your Hebrew pronunciation is getting better every time."

"Well, ya gotta *hauck* when you say it," I say. I nod at the television. "Put on the Passover episode. I don't know about that holiday yet." Max nods and clicks through, and the episode begins to play. My eyelids are heavy, and I lean a bit more onto Max's shoulder, sliding my feet farther away from me on the couch...

And suddenly, with a quick intake of breath, I'm awake, and Max's living room is dark.

Chapter 21

I text Max the next morning, a Saturday where the marine layer hangs on too long, like the sky is hungover and realizes that Los Angeles needs a day to rest and recover from the stress of being a city full of people striving for something more. Maybe it's because I grew up here, in a valley full of parents who had hopes of being child stars or athletes, but I never felt that drive. Maybe that's why I settled for my boring marketing jobs instead of saving the rainforest, choosing to focus more on Pantone color spreads instead of carbon dioxide in the atmosphere.

Brooklyn: I have a semi-regular thing I do on Saturday mornings. Want to join?

Max: I'm not doing a Soul Cycle class.

Brooklyn: It's cute that you think I can afford that. No, it's a volunteer thing.

I send him the pin along with a time and a suggestion to wear shoes he can walk in. I haven't seen him in athletic gear since the day we went ice skating. When we established boundaries that feel like they've grown taller by the day, even as the foundations crumble. Touches have grown longer and more frequent. Max likes to press his lips to my knuckles after I've made a joke, a tacit acknowledgment that he thinks it's funny, along with a quirk of his lips. When we sit at restaurants or the bar with my coworkers, he'll put a hand on my thigh, while I like to play with the hair at the nape of his neck.

It's all too much and not enough.

My brain needs a break from the office, from performing this relationship and the stress of analyzing what everyone is saying for some kind of double meaning. I haven't been to the shelter in a few months, not since I started at ConservTech, and it felt *right* when I woke up this morning. I logged on to their website and booked two volunteer slots, even before I asked Max.

Max beats me to the shelter, so I crack a joke about teleportation when I pull my car in next to his. He rolls his eyes and pulls me into a hug, his familiar scent of *something* wrapping around me like a blanket.

"I needed a break from the office," I say into his chest. "This is something I started doing in between jobs a few years ago."

He laughs, a puff of air against my forehead. "When I looked up the address, it made sense. It's so you." I pull my chest away, still keeping my arms wrapped around him, and give him a questioning look. "It's making the world a better place, in a little way. Classic Brooklyn." He leans down and presses a kiss to my forehead.

"We don't have to," I say. Because we're not in front of any of my coworkers, not wrapped up in business dress or evening wear. I'm wearing a pair of leggings and a T-shirt, with a sweatshirt from a concert I paid an arm and a leg for zipped over it. Max is back in joggers and a long-sleeve tech shirt from a 5k or a half marathon or something. His thumbs poke through the sleeves again.

"Maybe I wanted to," he says, more to the smog-filled breeze than to me. We let go of each other, and a moment of awkward silence passes before I lean my head toward the concrete block building.

"C'mon," I say, leading him forward. The shelter has the same smell as always, the same one that greeted me when my stepdad agreed to bring us here to get a dog when he moved in with us. It's antiseptic, wet dog, and a faint hint of cat litter. I'm greeted by a smiling woman. Today, her braids are in a bun on top of her head and she has a beautiful swipe of red glitter against the dark brown of her cheek as a holiday highlight.

"Brooklyn!" she says, giving me a wave.

"Hey, Deondra," I reply, grinning.

"Been a while."

I cringe. "I know. New job. Life shit."

Her eyes bounce between Max and me. "Is this the life shit?" She grins when Max goes a delightful shade of red, high up on his cheeks.

"Deondra, this is Max." He gives a bashful wave and doesn't say anything about how I've been purposefully vague about who he is to me.

"Cats or dogs today?" she asks, clacking away at her computer.

I turn to Max. "Are you a cat person or dog person?"

"Guess." He tucks his tongue into the corner of his mouth. He's being purposefully obstinate, which is usually how we fake flirt in front of our coworkers. Or at least I thought it was fake. The way Max is looking at me here, though, feels real. It feels like we're at that point in a relationship where the line between what is a date and just being around each other has blurred, like there's the expectation that we just *do* things together.

I bet he'd be a pain in the ass to go grocery shopping with. I bet he makes a list of everything he needs and compares the relative merits of brand name versus generic.

I get a twinge in my stomach at the idea of finding out.

"Well, *you're* the human embodiment of a cat, so I'm betting cats," I say, and Max's grin confirms that I'm right.

"And you're a dog person," Max says, also correct. "You go for the shy dogs, though, the ones that need a bit of extra love and attention. I bet you like to help them warm up to people so they're ready for their families."

Deondra's laugh saves me from asking how Max can do that, can see into my soul in such a casual manner. "He's got your number. There are a few sweet pitties that could use a game of fetch—you up for taking them out, Brooklyn?" I nod, and Deondra turns to Max. "All right, cat boy, have you ever volunteered with us before?"

"No," he says.

Deondra's face falls. "Well, we need a volunteer application and proof of a negative TB test before we can let you in."

Max smiles, tapping on his phone. He turns the screen to her. "There's my last TB test. I got it a year ago, so it's still valid. I submitted a volunteer application this morning, so it should be in your system." Because of course. Of course Max looked up what he needed and already took care of the paperwork. Because of course he's the kind of person who keeps test results on his phone, can find his vaccination records and other medical information at the drop of a hat.

My brain wonders what other kind of test results are on his phone. Shit.

"Well, Mr. Prepared Cat Boy, how do you feel about cat socialization?" Deondra asks, and Max nods, even without asking what that is. I've never been near cats, with allergies and my love of dogs helping me out. "Perfect. Brooklyn, you know where to go to find all the dog walking and play supplies. Ask Nikki to get you the pups we have earmarked for you. I'm going to take him back to the cat area." I slide my sunglasses back on my face and walk through the maze of buildings in this county complex—all the same type of easy-to-clean midsixties functional buildings—until I find Nikki, the other volunteer coordinator. I get the first dog, a beautiful light gray seal of a dog named Prancer and take him out to the large dog run.

Popping my earbuds in, I restart the podcast I was listening to in the car. Two women, one a rabbi and one a recent convert to Judaism, talking about concepts that are important to Judaism. I started listening to it when I felt guilty asking Max what felt like basic questions—why can't you eat shellfish?—and after googling questions about Judaism sent me down a rabbit hole of different flavors of the religion or gave me a website that recounted historically inaccurate, horribly antisemitic conspiracy theories. Prancer and I play fetch for twenty minutes as Yaffa and Elle talk about the concept of a *mitzvah* and I reflect on how Max is a living embodiment of the concept.

"You done, boy?" I ask Prancer, who has come back from this run a bit slower but smiling, his tongue lolling out of his mouth. I clip his leash to him, then lead him back to his crate, rewarding him with a treat I snuck from the volunteer desk. A scratch to the nose, then another behind his ears, and a hug are the way I like to say goodbye to each dog, letting them know that someone is out there for them. The next dog, another bully mix named Holly, is even more energetic than Prancer and still learning the concept of dropping the ball after fetch. My entire hand and arm are covered in dog drool by the time she's returned and the podcast episode has ended. I boot up another, this one about the pernicious stereotypes about Jews in Hollywood that seems appropriate for where I live, and take a German shepherd named Kringle for a walk around the grounds.

I learn more about *mitzvots* and Elle, who converted after marrying her husband, tells a story about how she's set up a mitzvah tree each fall. Her two daughters put a leaf on the tree each time they do something good for someone else. A discussion about what good deeds are for is next—if they're for one's own personal glory and pride or if they're whispered into the wind like secrets, some small wish to make the world a better place.

I feel a little surge of pride thinking about my own work here at the shelter. I started here because I missed having a dog and couldn't afford a pet deposit. Not to mention the odd hours I worked at my first job and how I liked to go out for drinks after work. I just wanted to be around something soft, and I found that, contrary to what I thought, I loved watching these dogs feel comfortable and ready to find their homes.

Maybe that's what I'm doing with Max. We'll be here and form this bond and then I'll...what? Let him go? We're friends now, for sure, but there's that undercurrent of some kind of connection that keeps me up at night and causes a pulse between my legs. Someone who is a better person than me could probably settle for being friends, for telling themselves that just getting to have Max in their life was enough.

I'm not that kind of person.

If I can't have him after this, I don't know what I'll do.

But that's a problem for future Brooklyn, like sea level rise or interest rates.

Kringle and I finish the loop of the land surrounding the shelter, a dusty bit of chaparral that passes as "nature" in this part of Los Angeles. I fully expect Max to be waiting outside, covered in cat hair and frowning slightly. Or worse, holding a kitten. I don't think my delicate heart could handle that. But the parking lot is empty, as is the lobby.

"Did Max leave?" I ask Deondra, even though his car is still there. Maybe he had an allergic reaction to all the fur and has been life-flighted.

"I haven't seen him come out," she says, then gets a conspiratorial grin on her face. "So what's the deal with you two?"

"We're friends. He's helping me with something for work. He's..." I let my voice trail off and look behind her.

"Clear as mud," Deondra says, and I roll my eyes and flick my middle finger at her. "You know where the cat room is if you want to go find him." Giving her a half smile and hoping I have Benadryl or something in my car, I follow the smaller paw prints painted on the floor to the room. I give casual nods to the cats prowling around in their cages and still can't find Max. But then I turn the corner, and my heartbeat kicks up to a level that science can't trace.

He's sitting in a glass-walled room with a cat tree in each corner. Small kittens cling to every surface, some in balls of fur that seem to be made up of three or four. In the center, sitting cross-legged like a first-grade teacher, is Max. Max, who has his glasses low on his nose and is reading from a book.

Out loud.

To kittens.

I can't see what book he's reading, but I'm sure it's some journalistic classic that I've never heard of. I can't hear him through the glass, so I settle for watching his lips form around the words. His right hand idly reaches down and gives a kitten a scratch on the head, while another bumps its head into the corner of the book. He pauses and gives the kitten a tiny scowl. It's the same kind of look he gives me when I'm being purposefully difficult, a glare with no heat behind it. A giggle escapes my mouth, something that reminds me of when I was in middle school and sneaking around, trying to catch my sister and her boyfriend after dates.

Max looks up and sees me, and that scowl is replaced by a genuine grin, a little wave. He gestures for me to come into the room, and I shake my head and pretend to sneeze into an imaginary tissue. He tosses his arms up in the air in an exaggerated version of his normal behavior. The smile on my face matches his, and I can see his shoulders shake with laughter. He holds up a finger to me and mouths *just a second*, then goes back to reading to the cats.

Later, he'll tell me that he had to finish reading the chapter to them.

I head back into the lobby, sure that I can't watch another minute of this scene without throwing everything we've worked for away. I pull out my phone and the list of reasons I have to keep this up—the story, the chance to make a difference, the way that men like Aron need to, for once in their life, face some fucking comeuppance for the shit they pull—and I take three deep breaths, like in the yoga classes I used to pay too much to do. More breaths. My heart rate is just coming down when Max walks out, and it shoots back up again.

"Thanks for inviting me, Brook," he says, picking a piece of cat hair off his shoulder. He turns around and thanks Deondra for the work she does here, too.

"Any little kitties you want to take home?" she asks, and Max looks like a little kid for a second.

"I'd take all of them home," he says, then his eyes flit to me, "but Brooklyn's allergic, and that's not fair to her." Oh, right. Because in our fake dating scheme, we're at the point in our relationship that we should be talking about moving in. Deondra raises one eyebrow, and I know I'm blushing. Not because I'm embarrassed, but because, just for a moment, I feel guilty. It's one thing to lie to people at work, but Deondra is a volunteer coordinator at an animal shelter. Someone that I see regularly. I don't even think she knows what I do, which is fine by me.

We're saying our goodbyes when a thought I had while playing fetch pops into my head. "Hey, Deondra, who names the animals here?"

"Usually the volunteers and the staff that are here when they're doing the intake. Why? Do you like all the Christmas names? There are a few studies that say that animals that have seasonally appropriate or locally funny names, like sports teams, get adopted faster. Especially with the season—dogs named Rudolph get taken home quickly in December!"

My throat feels a little dry right now, so I swallow and pull up my courage. It's silly, to be nervous about something like this. It's not like I'm taking a huge stand at a protest or breaking up a fight. Still, I lick my lips, then say, "You know, there are other holidays in December. You should try to name dogs after those."

Deondra thinks for a second. "You mean like a cat named Dreidel?"

"Yeah, like that. Or maybe after the principles of Kwanzaa."

"I'll talk to our pet admissions coordinator," Deondra says, smiling. "But yeah, I think we should do that. Expand our holiday offerings." She sighs. "It would probably be better coming from you, though." She looks between us, the way her eyes bounce between her arm and mine highlighting the difference in our skin tone.

I push down that bit of guilt I feel. "Let me know what I can do to help. It's up to you." A wave goodbye, then I walk outside.

"That was really cool," Max says after a few moments.

"It's the least I could do," I reply. "It's not much."

"Not much is better than nothing, which is what most people do." He puts his sunglasses on and looks out over the mountains most people forget that Los Angeles has.

"Nice bit of improv out there," I say, desperate to change the subject. There's something that makes me squirm when Max compliments me, and I can never tell if it's discomfort or something *more*. And if I investigate what that *more* is, I'll ruin this entire thing before we get a chance to make a difference.

Max gives a dismissive snort, but with a smile. "We do a lot of brainstorming at my place. I meant what I said. I don't want to affect your allergies." He pulls his sunglasses down his nose to give me the same look he gave the kitten, and I swallow a nervous laugh. "When are you going to learn that I don't lie to you?"

My reply is silence and a small smile.

"I'll see you tomorrow for lunch?" Max asks, opening his car door.

Chapter 22

There are a million and one reasons I want to quit ConservTech, most of which have to do with the CEO being a narcissistic creep who is conning the government and taxpayers out of millions in environmental fees. But working on Christmas Eve—something I requested off during my onboarding—is the most recent addition to the list. Sighing, I look at the group text between my sister, my stepdad, and my mom and see the picture. This is the day we always had with my dad—Mom got Christmas Day, when she could swing it—and it feels odd to be missing our holiday gathering. I think back to how many times Max said he missed High Holy Days because he wasn't allowed to miss work or school and I feel guilty that it's taken me until my midthirties to experience the type of deprivation that is common to Max, his family. Rachel from data analysis. Probably dozens of other people in my life. I've never thought to question that their cultural calendar is different from mine until now.

Bah humbug, indeed.

Muttering something about the unfairness of feeling like a grinch on my favorite day, I decide that I will take every single snack and free drink I can in the office as a way of vengeance. Like a Nespresso can make up for lost time with my family, but still. The coffee machine has just stopped whirring when I hear voices.

Like I've been trying to do, I keep my head down and my ears open. It's Aron—of course he's here on Christmas Eve, probably using the slow day at the office to push through deals or something else that would make Max get that bit of rage in his eye that I find ungodly attractive.

Or, it seems, to corner me.

"Hi, Brooklyn," he purrs. A shiver runs down my spine, and I roll my shoulders back and try to remember that I've got my eye on bigger things.

"Hello, Mr. Callahan." I love the way his eyes flash when I refuse to use his first name.

"I've told you, call me Aron."

"Okay, Aron." I lean into his name. "What are you doing here today? I thought that being CEO would mean you get the holiday off."

He snorts a laugh. "Who gives a fuck about this stupid holiday?"

I'm a bit shocked. I've spent the last month attending every one of the Corporate Mandated Holiday Events, and he's always seemed like the epitome of saccharine sweet Christmas spirit.

And then it hits me. Just like his attempt at being seen as a feminist, just like how he paints himself as the savior of the environment, Aron's Christmas spirit is just another costume he uses to fool everyone. I'm furious again, because it fooled *me*, and I should know better by now. I should know that he's a fucking snake—I do—and still I gave up my favorite holiday. Because maybe I could make a difference.

Sliding my hand into my pocket, I take out my phone and pretend to check the time. Aron is still complaining about how people take everything so seriously these days and he can't say anything anymore as I quickly swipe to the voice memo app. I haven't used it before, but I've seen the way that Max uses it when we're brainstorming. He likes to have a record of his thoughts because he's a "verbal processor," whatever that means. I feel a buzz in my bloodstream that signals that all the pieces are dropping into place, that I'm finally at the right place at the right time.

"Is that why you do it?" I ask, dropping my voice into a husky tone that might be sexy. That's the one I'd use to pick up someone at the bar, the one I haven't had to use around Max to get him to look at me with heat in his gaze.

"Do what?" Aron asks, leaning one hip against the counter, taking a sip of the coffee that I know he's poured bourbon into.

"Lie."

"I don't lie." And it's different from when Max says it. This is a setup for another line from him. "I massage the truth to make it suit me."

"The truth?" Max and I have had many conversations about truth, as it relates to politics, religion. I know that truth, while it seems simple, is a fuzzy concept. But I also know that whatever Aron is thinking, it's sure as fuck not the truth. I take a deep breath and launch myself off the edge into Truth. "The truth about all the settlements you've given to female employees who suspiciously quit after you pay them attention for six months? The truth about how you pledge donations to a variety of causes, but recent accounting from all the nonprofits shows that none of them ever received donations from you? The truth about how you refuse to provide health care and salary increases to the lowest paid-staff members, who are predominately people of color, but your white staff receive unlimited vacation and bonuses?" His face is turning purple. I take a deep breath and release the final statement.

"Or is it the truth about what your recycling partner is actually doing just south of the Marshall Islands?"

At first, Aron is speechless. I know that no matter what, I'm out of a job now. This was the last chance I had to do anything, and I may have just fucked everything up. But Aron sets his coffee mug down, his face scarily motionless. "You think you're so smart," he hisses at me. "You think you're the first person to put two and two together and get four?" He laughs. "Nah, you're just a nosy bitch who doesn't know what's good for her. Wake *up*, Brooklyn. You're not special, and you're not smart. You are, however, out of a job, starting now. So now, tomorrow, you'll wake up just another cunt I've had the unfortunate pleasure of encountering, and I'll still be me. I'll still be the one who understands that there's no winning. We're not saving the world, because it's *fucked*. I'm selling the belief that we can save the world so I can make sure I get a lifeboat. I'm selling the nonsense belief that things can change, like people like *me* winning isn't baked into the DNA of this entire fucking country." He leans forward, hot breath in my face. "If you were smart, you'd take what you learned and use it to benefit you. No one else matters. We're born alone and we die alone. If you were smart, you would have let me fuck you and taken what I'd have given you like a dozen other women before you." He gives me a patronizing smack on the cheek. "You'll learn next time. Now get the fuck out of my building."

My heart is racing, and I nod. All of my strong and badass words have left me, and I'm left praying that my phone captured it. "Oh, and Brooklyn?" I turn around. Aron is looking me up and down. "The only loss is I didn't get to fuck you while you worked for me." Speechless, I sprint down the hallway and press the elevator button seven times. I have a target on my back, and now that Aron knows that

CORPORATE MANDATED HOLIDAY ROMANCE   167

I know everything, there's a part of me that thinks he's going to take what he can from me. The last thing I want is to be—

"Maybe I decided it wasn't too late for that, Brooklyn." I hear slow, casual, threatening footsteps in the hallway. *Fuck.* Come on, technology gods. I push the button again, praying for a Christmas miracle. The elevator doors open slowly, and I rush inside, slamming my fist against the door close button.

"C'mon, c'mon, c'mon," I whisper. The doors close, and I take a moment to breathe. It takes an eternity to hit the lobby, and then I run outside, and all I can think of is getting a hold of Max.

I know enough about journalism now to not put anything in a text message or an email. Staying up late and watching old spy movies tells me that I should use a pay phone right now, but a quick search on my phone shows that not even Reddit has an accurate map of the remaining ones, and I doubt there are any downtown. I call Max quickly, wishing I had thought ahead to use a code word. The spies working against the Soviets in last night's film would be so disappointed in me.

"Brooklyn?" Max says by way of answering. "Are you okay?"

"I'm fine, well, I mean—"

"You've never called me. Not once."

Think, Brooklyn, think. "I'm really horny!" I say, and then cringe as someone on the street looks at me. "And I need to see you." There's silence on Max's end of the line, and I know the face he's making, and then I actually do start to feel a bit of a tingle between my legs. Frustrating him is usually one of my favorite things, but right now, I wish he understood me better. "I need you. In person. Alone. *Now.*" I try to infuse my voice with a tone that says *urgent and not about sex*.

"Oh? Oh!" Max says into the phone, then drops his voice to a whisper. "Now?"

"Yes, and not in public. Are you home?"

"I can be," he says in a rush. I hear the noise of a notebook being closed, a computer being closed. "I'll be there in five minutes."

"Leave the door open," I say, getting into my car and opening up my map app. When I go to enter Max's address, I notice that it's the automatic suggestion for where I go directly from leaving my office. I try to ignore how happy that makes me, how something shakes in my stomach like a snow globe.

I look at my phone and pray that I saved the audio correctly, then cut into traffic. I'm even bold enough to take the HOV lane, even though it's just me. Me and the recording that could break this story wide open.

Chapter 23

I PAY AN ABSOLUTELY absurd amount of money to park in the garage next to Max's building. I slam my car door, lock it, and run down the stairwell in the parking structure, looking over my shoulder every three steps. Logically, I doubt Aron followed me, but there's a part of me that might be worried every single time I step foot in this city from now on. I hit the sidewalk and turn toward Max's building.

"Brooklyn!" There's a moment where I think *shit, Aron did follow me*, and then I realize it's Max. Max is waiting outside his building, and I sprint over to him. Without pretense, he opens his arms, and I fold myself into them. He wraps his arms around me, and that small bit of comfort, of stability, unlocks the tears. I sob into his shoulder for two seconds before he says, "Can we get you inside?"

"Please," I breathe into his chest. He gives a squeeze, then slides his hand down my arm and grabs for my hand, wraps it in his, and pulls me in the lobby. The doorman gives us an odd glare, but it's Los Angeles, so I can't be the only sobbing woman he's seen come in here. Not for the first time, I wonder how many people Max has brought home.

He's patient, at least for Max, waiting until the elevator doors close before he turns to me and gives me a stern look. "Are you okay?"

"I think," I say, nodding.

"He didn't hurt you? Touch you?" Max's eyes bounce around my body, even though the real hurt is to my pride, to my emotions.

"No." I open my mouth to elaborate about how I think he wanted to when the doors open. Max pulls me into his apartment and sets me on the couch. He doesn't ask if I need anything. Instead, he's a small tornado rushing around—*here's a glass of water, Brook*, then a bag of Goldfish is thrust into my hands with an admonition to *eat, dammit. You need food*. He's boiling water for tea and rummaging in his cupboard. *I need the one with the bear; it helps calm me down*—when I finally interrupt him.

"Max!" I call. He slams the door shut. "I recorded him."

"You what?" He crosses over in what seems like two steps and sits next to me on the couch. Closer than when we usually work. Close enough that I want to reach out and take his hand.

And fuck it all, I do. I interlace my fingers with Max and awkwardly pull out my phone with my left hand. "He said something, and I just got so *fucking* angry. And I remembered that app you use when we talk and—" My left pointer finger is trembling as I press play. It's faint, but when I click up the volume, Aron's voice is clear and distinctive.

"Is that enough?" I ask Max, but he shushes me, intently listening to the rest of the recording. It doesn't so much end as it peters off as I storm out. Then all you can hear is my heavy breathing as I wait for the elevator. Max is quiet for a moment before he places his other hand over mine.

"You brilliant sneak," he whispers.

"Yeah?" I breathe.

CORPORATE MANDATED HOLIDAY ROMANCE 171

"We fuckin' got him." And then Max is back in motion, looking for his phone. He swipes through and taps out a text, hits send, then looks at me. "Can you spend the night?"

I've imagined Max asking me that more times than I'm comfortable admitting, but my answer is the same in this situation. "Of course. What can I help with?"

"You can make yourself tea, then we'll finally write this damn story."

But I can't focus on writing, I can't focus on anything but the fact that— "Does it matter anymore?" I ask, hoping that the desperation in my voice isn't a turnoff. "Tomorrow, I won't have a job. You won't be writing the story anymore. We'll just be Max and Brooklyn, two people who intersected in each other's lives."

"Brooklyn and Max," he corrects.

"Why?"

"You should get the primary credit for this story," he says, circling his hands around my waist. "This wouldn't have been possible without you."

"And you," I add.

"You're selling yourself short, my little journalist." He presses a kiss to my cheekbone. "We're a good team."

"One more night as a team, then," I whisper.

"One more night." He looks down at me, and then whispers back, "Merry Christmas, Brooklyn." Before I even have a chance to argue that he doesn't need to celebrate a holiday he doesn't care about, even after all of this nonsense, he steals the breath from my lungs with a kiss.

Chapter 24

I have replayed every single interaction between Max and me over the past two months. Every touch, every look, every kiss. When it's late and Gemma has turned off the TV and we've both headed to our respective bedrooms, I keep replaying those kisses, turning them into something more, as I slip my hand down my body and make myself come. I have imagined a million different endings to the kisses—the shelves in that storage room are much stronger in my imagination than in reality—but nothing has come close to this.

I find out that Max has been holding himself back in our previous physical interactions. He was all gentle touches and light kisses, perhaps a hint of strength in his fingertips that one time. But Max is *everywhere* right now, pressing me back into the couch with a strength that is surprising unleashed from his lithe form. He presses rushed kisses down my neck, to the collar of my shirt, and then back up to my ear. He takes the lobe in between his teeth and gives it a sharp tug, resulting in a pleasurable moan from deep in my core.

"All this time," he whispers in my ear, the sound waves from his voice causing every hair on my body to stand on edge. "All this time, you were always thinking. Always doing."

"Well, I-I mean, anyone would—" I begin to say, but he sits up, looking a bit wild, his hair tumbling in a thousand directions.

"No," he says, giving me a look that is so serious and quintessentially *Max* that I can't help but giggle. "No. No one else did. Just you." He stands up and holds his hand out. I slip mine into it, and he pulls me close. "Just you, Brooklyn." My mind thinks of a million other scenarios that he could use those words to refer to.

"Are we?" I ask, running my hand down his side, below his belt, and pressing my palm into where he's hard. I want to feel that hardness against my back, against my tits, in my mouth. Inside me, in my soul, where Max has slipped into the crevices, all wry smiles and cynical optimism.

"If you want to," he replies, his eyes rolling back slightly as I give a gentle squeeze.

"You did say we make a good team," I joke, and he looks at me again, then replies sternly.

"Let's see what other arenas we can transfer our skills to." And then he's kissing me again, but while he walks me backward toward his bedroom. The one place I have been *good* and not snooped in, no matter how many nights we've worked or written here. I had already dragged him into my mess; the least I could do was keep my mess out of his space.

He flips me and presses me against the door, his erection hard against my belly, grinding up into the softness of my stomach. I expected him to carry that same cynicism into bed, to be quiet and let me fill in the silences the way he does in our conversation or on the fake dates we've been on. When I imagined us together, when I allowed my mind to wander as my hand did, I spent the entire time working for his approval.

Turns out, that's not it. It's not the reality at all.

"Fucking shit," he mutters as I work his belt buckle. "Brooklyn, you're amazing, you feel so good." It's a stream of his thoughts coming directly from his brain to his mouth, and I crave more of it. I begin to lower myself to my knees, but Max shakes his head. I stand back up and rest my hands on his hips. "Bed, you beautiful creature," he says, kissing me again. "You, in there. Give me a minute, and I'll join you." He gives me another *Max* look and adds, "Less clothing than what you're wearing now." He nods in the direction of the bathroom. "I'll be in there, getting everything, and then I'll be ready. I need time to cool down, to get my head on straight."

He presses a hard kiss to my lips. Then, with a grunt, he heads into the bathroom. I open the door to the bedroom, half expecting a turn-of-the-century newsroom, and am slightly disappointed to find that, well, it's just a bedroom.

But it's Max's bedroom, and I'm here with a specific purpose in mind. I had a job to do.

I do an awkward spin, taking in the totality of the space. Some things are exactly what I expected—dark blue comforter, bed made, a stack of serious-looking books on a bedside table. But there are other, more surprising things. A photograph of Max and his sister laughing on a beach. A signed hockey jersey emblazoned with the number 13. I hear a noise from the hallway and remember that I'm supposed to be wearing less clothing—I really need to get better at remembering instructions when I'm supposed to be sneaking around. I quickly shuck off my leggings, wishing I had worn underwear that wasn't so damn seasonal. I've just reached for the hem of my sweatshirt when Max appears in the doorway.

I didn't turn on the overhead light, just the one on the bedside table, and he's backlit from the light in the hallway. I can make out the slight definition of his arms as he grips the doorframe. As he spreads his legs a touch wider, I can see that he's not wearing anything. And, if I'm taking it all in correctly, Max is definitely ready for what is going to happen.

"Brook," he jokingly chastises. "At least you did take off some clothes."

"I didn't know if you wanted all of them off," I whisper, my throat dry. Max is walking toward the bed, and I do my best to take him all in. He's proportional and wonderful and so damn sexy, but still *Max*.

"Honestly, I'd prefer for you to never wear clothes again." He chuckles.

"Stop." I laugh back, reaching for my shirt again.

"Let me," he says. Max places his hand over mine and tugs it away, presses a kiss to my knuckles. "I've been an idiot."

"Why?" I'm proud of my ability to form questions as he skims the fabric up my stomach.

"Because you always ask if I'm serious when I say nice things about you." My sweatshirt is off and then, quickly, my shirt and my most comfortable bra join it on the floor. Max presses a kiss to my sternum, a place I don't think any man has ever touched before, then slides his lips over to a nipple. A quick lick that sends me shivering before he pulls back and looks at me. "If my words aren't working, I guess it's time that I show you." He gives a gentle push on my shoulder, a suggestion for me to lie back. His pillows smell like him. Clean. Fresh. Pure.

There is nothing pure, though, about what he's mumbling as he crawls his way down the bed, his fingers running along the outsides of my thighs. The litany of praise stops when Max gets to my waistband, and he laughs.

I groan. "I know, I know. I clearly didn't think about this when I—"

"No, no, no," he laughs, and I can feel his breath on my core. He gives me a kiss just below my belly button. "I've never gotten a Christmas gift before, so I feel like this is perfectly wrapped for me." He looks up at me, brown eyes glittering. "Can I?"

"Please," I reply, lifting my hips as he slides them down.

"Do you usually beg for people to unwrap presents?" The underwear lands in the pile.

"I do when I'm the gift." I cringe. "Wow, that was so horrible."

"I liked it." He runs his hand up my inner thigh. "I like you." And then he presses his mouth to me lightly. "I think you're funny." A kiss to the crease of my hip. "You're sneaky." A lick. "You're passionate." Another kiss, this time on my clit. "You don't put up with anyone's shit." He licks again. "You're pretty." A laugh against me. "That's not specific enough. I love the way your eyes change when you're angry. I go mad for the way you bite your lip when you're lying." Lick. "I like the way you're wet for me."

With each sentence, I open to him more, my knees growing heavy and my hips moving more and more. Max keeps a light drag of his knuckles along the inside of my thigh, a grounding touch, as I shoot higher and higher. He keeps his teasing rhythm, now murmuring something about how I make him so frustrated it turns him on.

"Max," I pant. He keeps his focus, so I close my knees slightly. He looks up, a bit annoyed. I love it. "*Maxim*."

"Brooklyn?" His lips shine with my wetness as he smirks.

"Stop playing with me."

"Oh?" He runs one finger up and down, up and down. "What do you want?"

This man is the most infuriating, and I've never had this much fun in bed. I've never felt so *seen*. "I want to come."

"*Oh*," he says, nodding. With a grin, he slides his middle finger in, and then he's back on me. It takes about seven seconds of determination on Max's part for me to become untethered.

Max pulls back as I come down from my orgasm and watches a shiver run through my entire body, a satisfied grin on his face. I've seen it before, when he uncovers something or puts two pieces of a story together. It's *pride* and it's sexy as hell. He grabs a pillow from the side of my head and quickly wipes his face on it. He flips the pillow over and lies next to me.

"Wait," I say, rallying energy from some kind of reserve I didn't know I had. "You're done?"

"You want another one?" Max's hand crawls down my leg.

"Yeah," I say, taking his hand and intertwining his fingers with mine. "With you, Maxim." He gets a soft smile when I say his full name.

"Oh, well." He rolls his eyes. "I can probably do that." I raise my eyes at his erection and, to emphasize my point, reach down and wrap my fingers around him,

"Excellent." I stroke a few times, enjoying the way his eyes go a bit glazed. I get up on my knees and begin to head down to blow him, but he grabs my wrist and tugs me forward.

"No," he says, but it's a question. "I want to see you." He reaches for a moment and finds a condom, rolls it on. I appreciate that there's not a question about protection, but something we're tacitly agreed to. Even though my IUD can prevent a baby I'm not sure I can afford, I don't want to deal with anything else. He adjusts himself just so and motions for me to come up. It's a bit awkward, but my knees land on either side of his slim hips, and he runs his fingers along my rib cage.

"Yeah?" I ask, reaching down and notching him against me.

"Yes," he hisses.

I ease myself down, the stretch reminding me that it's been a while since anything has been inside me that wasn't silicone. Max keeps his hands on my hips, guiding me up and down with pushes of his fingers until my hips rest against his.

"Fuck, Brooklyn." Max looks like he's in the best kind of pain. "I"—he lets out a shaky breath—"I need a moment, but can I touch you?" Even though we're joined, Max has his hands a millimeter away from my chest.

"Please," I beg again. He's on me then, softly molding his palm around each breast. He angles his fingers, pinches each nipple and tugs. I moan and clench, which results in Max's hips punching up.

"Yeah?" he asks, tugging again.

"Mm-hmm" is my garbled phrase. It's not a heated, sweaty pumping of hips. I'm rocking, feeling that telltale pressure build again as Max lists all the things he's dreamed of doing with my tits and his mouth.

"Use me," Max says, his hands moving back to my hips. One thumb finds my clit and rubs. "All I want is for you to use me to come."

With that bit of permission, I begin to chase the orgasm with encouragement.

"Brooklyn, I'm close," he whispers, and his admission gets *me* near the edge. When his hips thrust up one more time, I'm over the edge. I collapse against him as he pulses inside of me, grunting in my ear. There's a moment of quiet where our hearts are beating, and I think there might be steam coming off our sweaty bodies.

"That's not all you want," I whisper to the side of his neck.

"Yeah?" he whispers back.

"You also want a Pulitzer." Max lets out his full laugh and kisses me hard.

After all appropriate post-coital chores are taken care of, I head back to Max's bed, where he's opened his laptop, the screen bright.

Max hits *send* on the email to three editors and sends a text to each of them, confirming that they've gotten the story. He glances at the time, then laughs.

"Merry Christmas," he says. It's 12:11 a.m., December twenty-fifth.

"Did you know that this is a traditional Christian holiday," I say in the same teasing, lecturing voice he used.

"You hungry?" He gets up and stretches, and I grin at the faint red marks on his stomach from my nails.

"Uh, of course," I reply, leaning into my Valley Girl accent as I follow him out of the room. "Like, what about taking down an evil billionaire doesn't get you, like, totally starving?"

Max is shaking his head, and I know what face he's making as he opens the refrigerator. He gets out a few takeout containers. "I caved yesterday and ordered my Chinese food early." He flips open a box and munches on something. "You see, I've had this *thing* for this woman and I was stressed about it, so I need rangoons."

"Sounds like you should have also gotten sweet and sour chicken." I let out a squeal of delight when he opens another box to reveal the bright red sauce over lumps of chicken and rice.

We snack and chat, each of us giggling like it's the first time we've ever kissed someone else, like we're a real couple, like the Christmas magic inside this bubble we're in will last for the rest of the season, maybe the rest of time.

Eventually, we make our way back to bed and fall asleep telling each other what we'd name a cat.

At four a.m., I'm sound asleep when Max's phone rings. It's the theme song from *The West Wing*, which I make fun of as he rolls over and grabs his phone.

"Shut up," he mumbles, and I cling to him like a koala. I glom onto his back while the bright light blinds us both. I blink before the screen comes into focus. He doesn't even try to prevent me from seeing it. Just three words.

We'll run it.

I don't even care what newspaper or website will run it or what the payment is—the story will be out there. It started as this tiny idea, an inkling that I had one day, and now it has spiraled, in the best ways, into an actual story. People I don't know will read it. It's real.

I look up at the ceiling, letting the adrenaline course through my body when Max wraps himself around me. "Do you get it now?"

"What?"

"Journalism." I make a noncommittal noise, and he continues, whispering like someone might overhear. "The way you know you've made a difference. That the story—the truth—is out there."

"It's intoxicating," I whisper, then laugh. "That's cheesy."

"That's beautiful," he says, but I notice he's looking at me, taking in my naked body, half uncovered by blankets in the light of his cell phone. A part of me wants to seize this moment, jump off the cliff. New Brooklyn would do that—

But Old Brooklyn still has to deal with the consequences. Find a job. Help her friends. I've changed a little, but I'm still me.

So while I want to tell him that we've got something special and that I might care about him in a way I haven't cared about anyone else, I know that I still have to protect myself. And Max.

"Max," I whisper. "I can't."

"Can't what?" His voice is resigned, like he knows it, too.

CORPORATE MANDATED HOLIDAY ROMANCE 181

"This is going to change your life," I say. "You're going to break one of the biggest stories this year."

"I couldn't have—"

But I stop him.

"I want this for you. I want everyone to know that Max Matuschansky"—I know I say it right, because he grins at me—"is the best damn journalist in California, the US, the world. But there's going to be fallout. And I think we have to weather that independently."

"What if I want to be by your side during it?"

I give a soft smile. "What I want and what I need to do are two very different things." I press a kiss to his chest, then the tip of his nose. "I need to know that I can process this on my own and figure out who I am in this new era." He wraps his hand around mine and I know him, my Max. I know he knows I'm right, because there's no questioning or poking holes. Just a kiss to my knuckles.

"I have the utmost confidence in you, Brooklyn Peters." He takes a breath, then opens his mouth, but I kiss him before those words can slip out. The kisses turn to sighs and then moans, and we come together again, then fall asleep, still as close as we could be.

We're awakened again when Max's phone rings. Early teasers of the story have gone out after an overnight fact-checking. He sits in bed, scrolling and pulling his hair, while I shower and pull on the same clothes I wore the night before. Ostensibly, I'm still Brooklyn, but I know I've changed.

I've helped break a story.

I've fallen in love.

I'm leaving.

"I'll talk to you soon?" I say, slipping on my shoes.

"Can I cook you breakfast, or we could go to the diner—"

"No, Max. I appreciate it, but I want you to bask in your glory today."

"Text me when you get home?" He looks hopeful, like there's a chance I might stay. I want to, but I know I have to leave.

"Of course."

Chapter 25

I SPEND THE NEXT two weeks in my apartment.

Instead of spending New Year's Day laughing over champagne with Vee and Carlina and kissing Max at midnight, I fall asleep on the couch watching rom-coms from high school. Gemma offered to stay home with me, but I saw the way her eyes lit up at a text message she received around nine p.m.

"Seriously, *go*," I told her as she was working on the buckle of a pair of strappy high heels. "Go get a kiss at midnight and channel all the best luck for the new year." I took a sip of Sleepytime Tea (with a splash of bourbon) I made for myself. "God knows I need it."

"I love you, Brooklyn," Gemma says.

"Who are you headed out with? Anyone I know?"

Gemma flushes a deep red. The color is at odds with her dark brown hair that's been streaked with pink. "Uh, you do know her, actually. Remember your old coworker, Rachel?"

I laugh into my mug of boozy tea. Rachel, the stunning woman who told off an entire holiday party, who I thought would be the perfect partner for Max, is going on a date with my roommate. The woman who once dated Max's sister. I'm always surprised how *small* Los Angeles can be once you get into your tiny niche. "She's gorgeous," I reply, instead of telling her the entire story. "She's Jewish. You know that, right?"

Gemma gives me that sad smile, the one people give you after you've been fired or broken up with, which is odd, because I haven't exactly experienced either over the past week. "I know, Brook." She grabs her purse. "Happy New Year."

I fell asleep to Heath Ledger singing to an entire football stadium and wake up sometime around four a.m. drooling on the couch cushions. Nothing has moved much, which means Gemma is ringing in the new year in a much more enjoyable style than I am. I pat around for my phone and find that it tumbled onto the floor. Walking into the bedroom, I look at my messages. The screen of my phone is almost painful with its brightness.

A photo of Carlina and Vee, their arms twisted together, pouring Miller High Life into each other's mouths. The accompanying message reads *Missing our third. Happy New Year, you sneaky bitch.* A photo of Gemma and Rachel kissing in front of the Taco Bell Cantina in Hollywood. A text from Gemma that says *not the only tacos I'm going to be eating tonight.* The standard Happy New Year with emojis from my mom and stepdad in the family thread.

And a message from Max. A selfie of him, on his couch (because I know that couch well), drinking from a small bottle of champagne.

Max: Happy New Year, Brook. I miss you.

Max: L'shana tova

Max: (even though OUR New Year already happened)

As corny as it is, I whisper *l'shana tova* to my phone, trying to practice my accent like Duolingo tells me. I send back a simple *Miss you, too*, which does not encapsulate one tenth of the things I feel about Max. I lie back on my pillow, then add *This is going to be a better year*.

Chapter 26

I MAY HAVE THOUGHT it was going to be a better year, but it certainly doesn't look that way on January first on the western calendar. I spend most of the day hiding in my room, ignoring invitations for New Year's brunch from Gemma and Rachel, though Vee does send me a custom cookie. The icing on the cookie says, in ridiculous script, *the rich*, and the card that accompanied says *you damn well better eat this*, which did make me laugh.

I'm not allowed to apply for jobs, on the advice of my stepdad's friend who has agreed to give me legal advice. In exchange, my stepdad has agreed to do a bunch of random chores around his house. I get a text from Max on January third, with a link to the *LA Times*.

It's running tomorrow. Here's the early edition.

I scan the article, not ready to relive the farce and horrible things Aron and Zane did. While the main story is the illegal dumping and aggressive carbon emissions that ConservTech lied about, not to mention the abuse of taxpayers' money, the secondary story is the string of NDAs Aron had women sign. A few days after Christmas, I forwarded an email I received to Max. The subject line read *Going on Record*. I could have called him, written that story myself, but I never felt right being the one doing the reporting.

That story, coupled with the number of sexual assault allegations that were "settled out of court," caused the Los Angeles public defender's office to open a full investigation against Aron. I don't have much faith in the American legal system, but at least all the accusers will have a chance to actually confront him in court. And, as Max liked to remind me, all of those testimonies are public record. There is no way Aron's reputation isn't ruined after this.

The other thing I scan the article for is my name. It's not there. Not even when I log on to Gemma's laptop and do a search for my name on the *LA Times* website, and then a general Google search. Right now, no one can trace my professional record with ConservTech, other than a single listing on my LinkedIn.

It's exactly what I wanted, and I'm still let down.

So I engage in the traditional mourning ritual of white women from the San Fernando Valley.

I *wallow*.

I lock myself in my room, only leaving to grab food delivery from the front door and to use the bathroom and maybe shower. I exist on a diet of Thai food, overpriced pints of ice cream, and past seasons of Bravo reality shows. At least I can enjoy their social downfalls instead of reflecting on how my own career is in the toilet.

For about a week, I subsist on take out and reality television. Gemma drags me out to the couch one day, where we mainline an entire season of *America's Next Top Model* and point out all the ways our generation is fucked in the body image department and I re-evaluate my teenager crush on Nigel. I fell asleep on the couch last night and woke up to Gemma holding out a cup of coffee.

"Brooklyn," she says, all stern.

"Yes?"

"I'm bringing Rachel over tonight. Which means you need to vacate the premises. Go for a walk. Touch grass, or whatever the kids say. Have you showered this week?"

"I've showered," I say, running my hands through my hair, dismayed to find out that it's greasier than I anticipated. "Okay, well, maybe not recently, but—"

"Brooklyn," Gemma says again. "Go shower. Put on clothes that aren't leggings and old Dodgers T-shirts you stole from me. Text someone to grab dinner."

"I'm still lying low," I argue, but she holds up a hand.

"Okay, fine. Then go somewhere and just be around people. Remember that the world is out there and you're making it better." She smiles at me, and I pull myself off the couch and wrap her in a hug. I pull back and wince, getting a whiff of my decidedly not fresh scent. "See? I told you."

I shower, which feels amazing, then wash my hair, shampooing twice like the bottle tells you to, even though you're not really supposed to. It's still cold in Los Angeles, so I put on a pair of tights and a sweater dress, something I would have called a holiday outfit a few weeks ago but now I just refer to as winter wear. I slide my feet into boots and put a headband on.

I try not to remember the way Max pulled the headband off and tossed it like a frisbee across his bedroom.

I've started a few text messages to him, but I don't have his skill with writing. Nothing I can say really communicates how grateful I am for him, how I miss his presence in my life, how I want to figure out what my next steps are alongside his. But we agreed that doing things on our own was the right step.

Doing the right thing sucks sometimes.

Gemma nods approvingly as I grab my keys from the front door. She's rearranging the throw pillows, then assessing the room with her hands on her hips to see if it sets the right mood. "Knowing you," I say, "those pillows will be on the floor in a matter of minutes." She smiles and gives me the middle finger. "What time can I come home? Will there be a sock or a scrunchie on the door?"

"I assume she'll spend the night, so can I text you when we head to sleep?" Gemma gives me a sympathetic look, and I realize how much she's done for me. She's made coffee every morning. She's helped with the laundry and trash and maintaining the apartment so I can just be sad. She's held me when I've cried and she hasn't forced me to talk about it. She's my best friend.

"Of course," I say, smiling. "I love you, you know that?"

She grins back. "I love you, too."

I drive around like gas isn't costing me half of my nonexistent paycheck and find myself winding up the roads to Griffith Park. I park at the observatory and spend a few minutes enjoying Los Angeles from above the smog. Thinking about the fact that there are a few people who can sleep easier and more small governments that will be able to pay more employees. I imagine the lights of the houses and skyscrapers are winking at me, telling me *good job*.

I drive down through Griffith Park, enjoying the peace and quiet until it gets to be a bit too much, then I maneuver back to Culver City.

I slide into a bar I like, one that feels cozy and unpretentious, which is harder to find in Los Angeles County than you'd expect. I'm fiddling with my phone, willing my fingers not to re-download social media or google Max's name or send him a message, when I start to eavesdrop on the group next to me.

Now, I used to actively try to *not* eavesdrop in public, but after spending a month and a half as an investigative journalist (sort of), listening to the world around me has become second nature. I realize that this is the way Max sees the world, not only looking for a story, but finding the beauty in the mundane. The fact that every person has a lifetime of stories and secrets that could potentially mean the world if put together like puzzle pieces.

I'm hoping for some juicy gossip, or a good sex story, or maybe some mindless corporate drama, but it turns out they're talking about podcasts. I laugh into my drink, imagining what Max would say about the changing popularity of modes of media.

"It's like, better than the original *Serial*," someone is saying, "because it's about white-collar crime!"

I think back to one of Max's rants about the popularity of the true crime genre and giggle again. And keep listening.

"I mean, I can't believe they're still producing episodes," someone else joins in. "The story keeps going and going."

"I can't believe I donated to that Aron prick's foundation," says a disdainful voice. "He really had me believing he was this progressive champion."

My heart skips a beat.

The first voice continues talking. "Have you been reading the long form articles, too? I mean, the podcast is great, but the articles are really where I've been learning a lot. I like that I can take my time with it, you know? Put the article down and come back to it or look back to a previous infographic."

I'm pretty sure I've stopped breathing at this point.

"The guy sounds cute, too," someone continues.

"How can a voice sound cute?"

"I dunno, but he does. He's like, nerdy and passionate and has this way of picking apart stories. Like, he explains all this stuff that's super complex, like shell companies and NDAs and tax shelters, and I *get* it." A laugh. "I wish he would have taught my high school econ class. Maybe I wouldn't have taken on so much student debt."

My eavesdropping is rudely interrupted when the voice that's speaking turns around and asks, "Uh, can I help you?"

I've lost any pretense of *playing it cool*, leaning over and inserting myself into their conversation. I'm leaning so aggressively I'm surprised I haven't toppled my barstool over. "Oh, sorry," I say, feeling my cheeks heat. "Just, what you're talking about sounds fascinating."

"You haven't been listening to it?" This from a man with broad shoulders and a beard. "Have you been under a rock the past month?"

He's oddly close to the truth. Do you think he'll believe that I was the source for the story and had to delete social media so I wouldn't be targeted? "Something like that." I pull out my phone. "What's the name of the podcast?"

"*Emet Weekly*," another responds, showing me the homepage on her app.

"Truth," I whisper and get a nod and a smile from a woman with curly black hair near the edge of the group.

"A chosen one," she laughs, lifting one corner of her mouth.

"Not exactly," I say, avoiding the conversation of why I know basic Hebrew. "You said it's not just a podcast?"

"Yeah, that's the coolest thing," says the woman who noticed I translated. "The podcast is kind of, like, secondary. You have to read the long form articles to even understand the podcast."

Someone else joins in. "Yeah, the host says it's a way of reclaiming the written word in journalism. But he provides an audio version for visually impaired."

"And a transcript of the podcast, too," she adds. "Hi, by the way. I'm Ruth."

"Brooklyn," I say, shaking her hand.

"Why are you so interested?"

"Other than wanting to eat the rich?" I chuckle. "The host sounds like someone I used to know. I like his perspective."

"I hope you enjoy it," she says, smiling and turning back to her friends. I quickly pull up the website and see that Max has published three articles so far, each longer than five thousand words. Scrolling through, I scan the art and diagrams and so much that is just so *Max*. So much so that the phone screen starts to blur in front of me.

After reading the first article and paying for my tab, I practically sprint to my car and fumble with my aux cord. It takes me three tries to properly put the cord into my phone, and then I hear it.

After a short little musical introduction, Max's voice fills my car. He completely surrounds me, just like on Christmas. Instead of whispering praise about my brain and my body, though, he's back to Serious Max, the one who could talk for hours about late-stage capitalism.

"Last week, we took you through the reporting on the financial loopholes that Aron and ConservTech used to hide the profits from their illegal dumping scheme," he says. I can see the tilt of his head and the quirk of his lips. I'm more than 100 percent sure that every time he gets to record one of these episodes, recounting *his* story, he feels it's another point on the side of good.

Chapter 27

Dear Max,

Longtime listener, first-time letter writer.

Does that joke translate to this medium? That's definitely not a question I would have asked myself two months ago.

I've spent the last week listening to every single episode of your podcast and reading your stories. Thank you for getting the story out there in a way that neither of us could imagine. Hearing your voice and reading your words has led me to one conclusion.

I miss you.

I miss the way your mind picks apart stories. I miss the way you're always a bit frantic. I miss the way you can never turn off your damn journalism brain and you've always got just one more question to ask me.

I want to finish the second story we started.

I want to start something new with you.

If you're free, there's a question I'd like to ask you.

You have my number, if you'd like to call.

Yours, always,

Brooklyn.

Chapter 28

My phone rings three days later. My impulse is to click the call away, but something makes me flip the screen over to see who it is. Maybe it's that thing with feathers that lives in my chest.

Hope.

The screen is lit up with a photo I snapped of Max during a brainstorming session at the diner. He was giving the *Max Face*, the one where he tries to look like he's angry but he's actually swallowing a laugh. I take a deep breath and answer.

"Brooklyn Peters speaking," I say in my best imitation of Max. He laughs back, and it's like warmth is being infused into my veins.

"Hey, Brook." The nickname is familiar. "I got your letter."

"I know it was silly, but I also know how much you value the written word—" I begin, but he stops me.

"It was perfect. You're, well..." A sigh. He's composing his thoughts. "I miss you."

"I miss you, too. I, uh, I listen to the podcast."

"I read that in your letter."

"Thank you for hiring Vee."

"It wasn't a favor. Their design work is amazing. I'm hoping to have Carlina do video soon." Max, always practical.

"You're good?" There are a thousand other questions in the subtext of that one sentence, but I've always been a bit tongue-tied around him.

"I'm good," he replies, then adds, "I'd be a lot better if you were around."

I chuckle a response. "I could probably make that work."

"What are you doing this Friday?"

"Crashing your Shabbat, I hope." I take a guess.

"Something like that. Can you be over around five?" It's before sunset, even this early in the year, but I know Max wouldn't have asked me if he didn't plan every single moment.

"Of course."

It's like Los Angeles is on my side tonight. It rained yesterday, so the smog has cleared, giving me a clear view of the Hollywood sign and the skyscrapers downtown. You can see the mountains that surround the city, the ones no television show or movie manage to capture just right. Even traffic is on my side—I can actually drive close to the speed limit as I drop into downtown, and not even the crumpled foil of the Disney Concert Hall can harsh my good mood. There was a time, just a few months ago, that I would have thought that everything lining up for me meant something horrible was about to happen.

But now, I even find a parking spot within two blocks of Max's apartment that has time left on the meter. I am unstoppable now. Reaching across the front seat of my car, I grab the bag containing a potato side dish I made with parmesan and za'atar seasoning. I'm sure Max will act like I didn't need to bring anything, but I want to show up with something other than myself. I don't know if this is the beginning of something new or settling back into a familiar friendship, but I've prepared for all scenarios.

And if there's a change of clothes and a toothbrush in my back seat, well, I can pretend that's for a separate occasion.

I walk down the street, even enjoying the smell of wet Los Angeles sidewalk, and begin to wonder if Gemma slipped something into my morning coffee. I walk into the lobby and take a deep breath. The elevator is strangely welcoming. I know this elevator. I know what it's like to be nervous in this space. I know what it's like to cry in this space. I even know what it's like to cuddle in this space, a gentle forehead kiss from Max as he walked me out to my car on the day after Christmas.

Max's door is undecorated, as usual. It's always been easy to pick out, no wreaths or lights. I'm about to knock, my fist held up, when Max opens the door.

And it's just Max. I expect to see Mai and Henri and Luis, but there's no one. Just Max.

Max, who always looks good, but who looks a different type of good. I didn't realize it when we were working on the article, but there was an edge of exhaustion around his eyes. They're soft now, and his cheeks have just a bit more color. He's in a soft-looking sweater, sleeves pushed up, and jeans I remember slipping my hand into.

"Hey, Brook," he says, smiling.

"Hi, Max," I reply. "*Chag sameach.*" I've been practicing the pronunciation, but the words feel thick on my tongue. It could be the way Max is looking at me, a combination of surprise and pride, like he can't believe I showed up.

"You've been practicing Hebrew?" he asks. I know there's another question hidden in that, but I'm not sure if I'm ready to admit everything to him. Yet.

"Listen, that owl sends me messages that make me feel so guilty. I know the owl means well and it's for my own good, so I can't let him down."

"Sounds like my mom," Max laughs. "Last week, on the phone, she asked me again when I was going to invite you over."

I follow him into his apartment where, as usual for Shabbat, it smells fantastic. Something like rosemary and cinnamon and savory-fresh. I spot two bottles of wine on the counter, both open, a red and a white, and I turn round and give him a confused look. "Am I early? Are we expecting more people?"

"No, it's just us tonight," Max replies as he pulls out the Pyrex dish wrapped in tinfoil. He opens the corner and takes a sniff, then gives me an approving smile. I wondered if I would still crave his small bits of praise after this break. The hammering in my chest tells me I still do.

"Do you plan on turning up tonight?" He gives me a questioning look, and, god *help me*, I do the least sexy thing in the world.

I quote the Black Eyed Peas.

"Fill up my cup?" I sing. "L'chaim!" And we're back to normal, Max giving me that disappointed-but-laughing look I love and me stifling a giggle as I try to look serious.

"Listen, that song taught a lot of Gentiles about Hebrew." He chuckles, then waves his hand. "No, it's for later. Unless you want a glass now?"

"Sure," I say, just for something to do with my hands that isn't grabbing Max by the sweater and seeing if he still tastes the same. Max gets out two glasses and pours a glass of wine from a third bottle, and I'm severely confused.

"Three bottles?" I ask as he hands me the glass.

"No, no, the others are for ceremony. It's a holiday today."

"It's always a holiday," I say, repeating a joke Max told me weeks ago. I make a face then, realizing it sounds different coming out of *my* mouth rather than his. "Sorry." I take a sip. "What I meant was, what holiday is it?"

"Tu B'Shevat," he replies, and I do my best to visualize how it looks spelled out. I haven't even tried to learn the Hebrew alphabet yet. Syllables are hard enough. I squelch down the hope that a future Max will teach future Brooklyn how to understand the curves and dashes. "It's not easy to exactly translate, but it's essentially the New Year for Trees. It's a minor holiday, but—" He blushes. "I wanted an excuse to do something special for you."

"Oh," I say, nodding. We're awkwardly standing two feet from each other, each holding glasses and taking sips in the quiet. Max opens his mouth at the same time I do, and we both try to start a sentence.

"You go," I say.

"You know I hate being first," he says, a sly twinkle in his eye that reminds me of how he told me weeks ago that he loves to make sure his partner is taken care of first. A flash of heat at the memory of experiencing it myself. I roll my eyes and make the decision to head over to the dining room table. Max joins me after a quick check of the oven.

"Thank you for coming over," he begins. "I hope traffic wasn't too bad—"

I hold up my hand to stop him with a laugh. "Max, we can't just talk about traffic like we're two Angelenos who have never met. We, well, we have history." He nods. "And you're a big famous journalist now!"

"I'm not famous," he says, but the blush high on his cheeks tells me he knows he's getting noticed.

"Is that Google alert destroying your inbox?"

"I had to turn it off," he admits. "It's been unreal. But Brooklyn, I couldn't have done any of it without you. I invited you here tonight to—" The buzzer on the oven interrupts him, and he quickly goes to check on the food again, muttering to the tinfoil. Then he comes back to the table. There's a moment where it's quiet and we just look at each other, wineglasses lightly held in of our hands.

New Brooklyn says things.

"I missed you," I say. "No, that's not right. I *miss* you. It's an active process and one I would very much like to stop," I say. The hand not holding my wine reaches halfway across the table.

"And here I thought I was the one who was good with words." Max laughs, and for a moment, I'm worried that I have misread the entire situation. But then his hand is soft on mine.

"I mean, I write mean copy," I joke back.

"Hell of a future as a journalist if you wanted it."

I take another risk. "I think I'd rather date a journalist instead of be one."

Max nearly chokes on his wine. "Really?"

I smile. "Yes, really. I actually like marketing. Especially if I could use it for something good. My blood pressure can't handle dipping another toe into journalism. But enough about what I like—which, just so I'm saying it very clear—is you. You can record me on that. I give you consent."

"Two-party consent state," Max says, smiling and remembering our first breakfast together.

"So one party consents. Do you? Max, do we make a go of this?" I've never been someone who puts herself out there like this, who boldly demands an answer of someone she cares so deeply for.

"Yes, Brooklyn. I consent." And then I get up from the table, still holding Max's hand, and pull him to me. We kiss like no time has been lost, like we're still sitting together and writing the story and joking about how corny Christmas traditions are.

Max breaks the kiss first and gives me *that* look. "You're always one step ahead of me," he says, frustrated with a current of affection.

"Hmm?" I ask, wanting to move from *less talking* to *more kissing*.

"Just wait. Lemme just..." He breaks off with a grunt I've learned means "let me show you because I can't explain." Still holding my hand, he brings me over to the counter where the bottle of red is open, though neither of us has touched our glasses. He drops my hand and opens the bottle of white, pours it into a glass.

"Okay, so add enough red until it changes color," Max instructs.

"Why?"

"Have a woman write *one* breaking news story, and she's all questions," Max jokes.

"I learned from the best." I press a kiss to his temple.

"To symbolize the changing of the seasons." I tip a bit into the glass, the pale yellow turning to a dusty pink. Max places his hand on top of mine and pours in a bit more. "To symbolize the start of something new." Setting the wine down, we kiss again. The oven beeps again, and I pull back.

"Is that the whole ceremony?" I ask while Max prepares our dishes.

"What makes you ask?"

"Well, it's just—" I'm still learning how to phrase things so they don't come out judgmental. "It's just that most Jewish ceremonies seem pretty *involved*."

"That's for next year," Max replies, setting the dishes down. "If you want."

"I want," I reply, picking up my fork. We eat and catch each other up on our lives over the past month, which mostly means I ask Max questions and he proceeds to get increasingly embarrassed about his new level of fame.

"Did I hear that *LA Weekly* is going to name you one of the city's sexiest journalists?" I joke as we scrape our plates and put them in the dishwasher, wrap up leftovers.

"That's not a real award, Brook," he replies, and goodness, I missed that nickname.

"I know. I just like getting under your skin. Plus," I hop up on the kitchen counter and kick my socked feet against the counter, "you'd definitely win sexiest journalist in my book."

"Hmm." Max comes over and fits himself between my thighs and wraps his arms around my waist, the tips of his fingers brushing the hem of my shirt. "I think you'd win sexiest undercover source."

"Sexiest male figure skater," I add.

"Sexiest karaoke queen," he replies. And then he kisses me, and all teasing is gone.

"Max, are you sure—" I begin, but he quiets me with a kiss and his palm on my ass.

"I haven't thought of anything but you since you left," he says, then cocks his head and reconsiders. "Okay, well, there's the whole *new phase of my career* thing, but you're around my brain a lot."

I giggle and slide off the cabinet, greedily pulling Max's shirt out of his pants and over his head. I'm grateful I wore a dress this evening, because one item of clothing is much quicker for Max to take off my body. We've somehow made it to the couch—Max shirtless, me in my underwear—and he pulls me on top of him, and I flash back to our first kiss. This time, I get to grind on him, the denim of his jeans and the lace of my panties providing the perfect level of friction.

"Yeah, Brook," Max encourages when he sees what I'm doing. "Chase it." And so I do, and I come, with Max's mouth on my neck. Slightly boneless, I'm easy to move when Max gets up.

"Condom," he pants and disappears for a moment, coming back entirely naked. "Off, off, get it all off." He waves a hand at me, laughing, and I comply, shucking the rest of my clothes.

He steers me over to the window and presses gently on my back so my forearms rest on the window ledge. We're high above the city. I can see the line of jets ready to land at LAX. I can see the streams of traffic.

Max is behind me, cock lined up against the curve of my ass. "Ready?" I nod. "You see that whole city?" He slides a finger in, checking, then all of him fills me up. I huff out a breath against the window, causing it to fog slightly. "You see it Brooklyn?" He thrusts, and I moan out a *yes*. "That whole fucking city is better because of you." Another thrust, and I'm panting against the window. He moves the hair off my neck and sucks at my nape. "You unlocked something better." I'm trembling, on the edge, so I slide a hand from the windowsill between my legs. "Touch yourself, Brooklyn. You deserve to feel so fucking good." I whine as my fingers slide through my wetness. Max continues, his hips slapping against my ass. I come again and regain the power of speech.

"You too," I manage to squeak out. "I can't do this without you."

"Damn right," he says. "It's *us*." I look in the window and meet his eye in the reflection. He's trembling, and I get the pleasure of watching him come with a *fuck, Brook* that has me pressing back, trying to wring all the pleasure for him.

He's a bit winded, and I'm a bit dizzy as he folds his lanky body over mine and wraps his arms around my chest. "Us," he says again.

"Us," I repeat.

Chapter 29

"You know, I didn't just invite you over to feed you and then fuck you," Max says after a few moments.

I lift up on my elbows and push my hair out of my eyes. "There's more?" I don't know how much more I can take.

"Yes, Brooklyn. I had this whole idea and symbolism and, well." Max is *pouting*. He just made me see stars, and he's pouting.

I'm so head over heels for him.

"How about I put on my dress again, and I'll be surprised? We didn't even make it to your bedroom, so does it even count?" I push back from the window, ignoring the red dents on my forearms from the ledge.

"That better count," Max says. "I'm almost as proud of that as I am of the story we broke."

"Hmm." I pretend to pout. "I'll have to do better next time." I run to the bathroom and take care of the necessary business, and when I come out, Max is washing his hands and putting on a coat. I grab my beanie and shove it on my head and hold out my hand.

Sliding his palm into my own, Max leads me down the stairs of his apartment and across the street. He stops at the bottom of the stairs and grabs a reusable shopping bag that's full of something, but he hides it to his side, clearly not wanting me to see what is in it. We cross the street and walk a bit farther, turning into a neighborhood park. Max is explaining how his mom spent a year living on something called a *kibbutz* and how she got involved in a variety of ecological projects when she moved back to Indiana.

"It's cool that you have had your own Earth Day for years. And you didn't need a massive oil spill or rivers catching on fire to care about it."

"Something that I've realized about Judaism," he says, slowing down and looking for something on the ground, "is that we honor the past by caring for the future." He pulls out a sapling from the bag, its roots wrapped in burlap. "I want to build a future with you Brooklyn. Not just a working relationship, not as friends." He swallows. "I care for you." He finds what he was looking for, a stake in the ground, and kneels next to it. I join him without question.

"I missed you," I say in reply. "I'm in."

He holds up the tiny tree. "It's cheesy as all hell, but my mom always had us plant trees on Tu B'shevat. Think about how we could use this holiday to make the air cleaner and revisit it each year." He looks up at me, the knees of his khakis already muddy.

"Are we going to visit this tree each year as we get older and it gets taller?" I joke. "I don't know if I want this tree to remind me of my impending mortality." He opens his mouth, but I gently place a hand over it. "Yes, I know. We die three times." I dig in the bag and find a small shovel and scoop a bit of dirt. "I like our tree."

"And yes, before you ask, I got this approved with the City Parks. It's a native tree and they know where I'm planting it." Max grins at me. I kneel down, and we busy ourselves with planting the tree. Max spends a few extra moments fussing with the dirt after because of an article he read about how to make sure it gets every drop of water it needs.

There's a moment of silence as we hold hands and look at our tiny sapling. I don't know what's going through Max's head, but I'm thinking of potential. Of the fact that this tiny twig can grow and make the air cleaner and provide shade for a kid who wants to read or even a place for a dog to take a piss. These small moments of joy and comfort remind me that, in spite of everything, there's no reason to give up. Max squeezes my hand, and I turn my gaze to him. My chest feels like it's going to burst.

I don't know what the future holds. I don't know what the world is going to end up like. But I know I want to make it better, and I know I want to do it with Max by my side.

Epilogue

"WAKEY, WAKEY, EGGS AND bakey!" I say, flipping on the light and holding a piece of turkey bacon out in front of Max's nose. He blinks open one eye and snags a bite of it before pulling me down for a kiss that is equal parts my coffee breath, his morning breath, and turkey bacon.

It should be disgusting, but it's not. Because it's a big day, and I get to wake up with My Max.

It's a soft, domestic morning—coffee and breakfast, then a shared shower that ends with both of us smiling. The domestic morning, however, is replaced with a rush of chaos starting at eleven. Max and I are both attending an awards ceremony for excellence in podcasting. I've rented a *gown* and Max, who is getting used to attending these types of events, actually owns a tuxedo now. He looks unfairly gorgeous in it.

"Hurry!" he calls from the living room. I'm in the bathroom, putting the finishing touches on my makeup. When I head to the living room, Max gives a low whistle, and I spin.

"You're my date to this?" he asks, fidgeting with his bow tie.

Max's podcast has been nominated, of course, but three podcasts from the network I manage are up for awards. Max likes to remind me that I have a better chance of winning than he does, and maybe I pretend to forget that so I can hear him tell me again and again.

"I guess so." I slip on my heels, then Max helps me up. "Are you ready to give a speech about the importance of actual journalists creating podcasts instead of a comedian interviewing his famous friends?" I tug his bow tie for good measure.

"I'll be good," he grumbles.

"Nah," I say. "It's more fun if we're honest."

Max and I dated for six months before we moved in together. I miss Culver City and its weird architecture, but I like his place more, and the view doesn't hurt either. Plus, Rachel moved in with Gemma, and she needed a home office for her new job, so it all worked out in the end.

What started as Max expanding on the reporting we did spiraled into another series—this one focusing on the ways that professional sports teams lie to taxpayers to get kickbacks in development. He has ideas for about seven more stories, and that's just what he told me last night.

Along with Vee and Carlina, Max started a new podcast network that combines long-form articles and detailed infographics and short documentaries with the shows. They're hosting three shows currently and are expanding all the time, partnering with locally owned smaller newspapers to provide more access and attention. I'm so unbelievably proud of him.

He offered me a job as their marketing coordinator, but I wanted to keep business and pleasure separate. But I like journalism, so I got a job with our local public radio station. Even so, there's something that pulls me towards the storytelling. I've started to spend a bit more time with the producers and even did the introductions to one episode. Turns out, journalism is more fun than corporate life.

He holds me at arm's length and looks me up and down. "I love you," he says simply.

"*Ani ohevet otcha*," I reply. While I haven't decided whether I want to convert, I've continued learning about Max's culture, even taking Hebrew lessons. I've learned how to braid *challah*, and Max has come to dinners with my mom and stepdad. He plays pickleball with my sister. I sat seder with his parents. We're building a life together, a family, that is. One of these weeks, we're going to include a cat, though we're still debating its name. I'm lucky that the radio station has good health insurance and I can get allergy shots. Because kittens are adorable, and Max with a cat does something to my insides I'm not proud of. But it's our life and these are our choices, and I know that we'll make them together.

It's perfect and a reminder that sometimes things do go right.

Acknowledgements

No one writes books alone, least of all this one.

Elle and Yaffa — for believing in me when I told you this plot and providing the most beautiful and introspective feedback. I'm so grateful for you in my life.

Anna and Emma –- for providing insights into other aspects of the Jewish and interfaith relationship experience. And for being two very cool humans who I get to call friends.

Ari Baran and KD Casey — not only writing some of the best sports romances out there, but for modeling the beauty of Jewish characters in romance. And for feedback. And for being author friends.

Megan and Kelsey –- for getting my into baseball and giving me something to distract my mind with. And for (Kels) designing the cover of my MCM dreams and (Megan) for believing in Brooklyn and Max early on.

Dani, Sarah, Eliza — my authors who lift me up and remind me that we are all in this together. I'm so grateful for your brilliance and continual friendship. And for that one night at Steamy Lit with the two corkscrews in one cork. I haven't laughed that hard in years.

And for any reader that believed in my stories and books — I am more grateful than you'll ever know.

And, as always, to Brady — the best Goodbye Earl singer there ever was.

About Nellie

Nellie Wilson is the pen name of a historian in her mid-30s who has an impossible-to-spell real name. Originally from western Pennsylvania, Nellie spent time in Ohio and Colorado before settling in San Diego with her partner and snaggletoothed dog. She enjoys drinking beer, talking about medical history and city planning, listening to emo music from the 2000s, and has recently started roller skating. When not writing books, she works as an architectural historian and reads Wikipedia entries for fun. You can find her on Instagram under @woahnelliewrites and occasionally struggling on TikTok under the same username.

Also By Nellie Wilson

Need S'more Time – June & Colin
A burned out teacher meets a camp director on a school trip. Can she evaluate her life in this new normal and make room for love?

Curated – Emmy & Ryan
A cynical historian and a sunshine paleontologist are thrown together professionally and romantically when their museums merge.

Storm Warning: A Novella – Violet & Julian
Two meteorologists who have a heated history with each other spend a summer chasing tornadoes.

Educated – Phoebe & Declan
Casual friends strike up a beneficial relationship that helps them both understand boundaries and what it means to do life with a partner by your side.

Coming Soon

Exhibited – Jeremy & Davis
(Early Spring 2024)
Mountain Friend Duology – 2024
Foster & ??
Flo & ??

Bold Will Hold
Lina & ????